THE ROYAL HOUSE OF NIROLI

Large Print Collection

SEMPRE APPASSIONATO, SEMPRE FIERO

Always passionate, always proud

The richest royal family in the world—united by blood and passion, torn apart by deceit and desire—now available in easier to read large print.

The Official Fierezza Family Tree

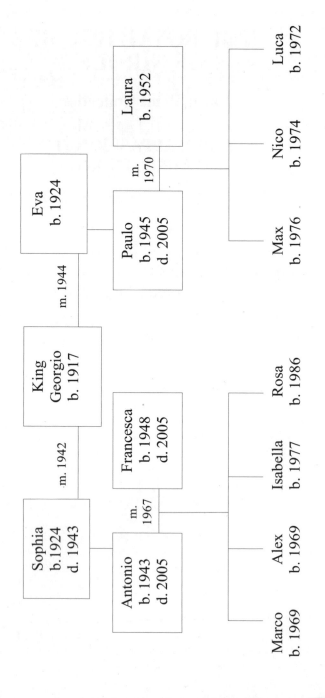

THE PRINCE'S FORBIDDEN VIRGIN

Robyn Donald

MILLS & BOON

First published in Great Britain 2007
Large Print Edition 2010
Harlequin Mills & Boon Limited,
Eton House, 18-24 Paradise Road, Richmond, Surrey TW9 1SR

© Harlequin Books S.A. 2007

ISBN: 978 0 263 21632 5

THE PRINCE'S FORBIDDEN VIRGIN

Special thanks and acknowledgement are given to Robyn Donald for her contribution to *The Royal House of Niroli* series

Printed and bound in Great Britain
by CPI Antony Rowe, Chippenham, Wiltshire

THE RULES OF
THE ROYAL HOUSE OF NIROLI

Rule 1: The ruler must be a moral leader. Any act which brings the Royal House into disrepute will rule a contender out of the succession to the throne.

Rule 2: No member of the Royal House may be joined in marriage without consent of the ruler. Any such union concluded results in exclusion and deprivation of honours and privileges.

Rule 3: No marriage is permitted if the interests of Niroli become compromised through the union.

Rule 4: It is not permitted for the ruler of Niroli to marry a person who has previously been divorced.

Rule 5: Marriage between members of the Royal House who are blood relations is forbidden.

Rule 6: The ruler directs the education of all members of the Royal House, even when the general care of the children belongs to their parents.

Rule 7: Without the approval or consent of the ruler, no member of the Royal House can make debts over the possibility of payment.

Rule 8: No member of the Royal House can accept inheritance nor any donation without the consent and approval of the ruler.

Rule 9: The ruler of Niroli must dedicate their life to the Kingdom. Therefore they are not permitted to have a profession.

Rule 10: Members of the Royal House must reside in Niroli or in a country approved by the ruler. However the ruler *must* reside in Niroli.

CHAPTER ONE

'ROSA! Telephone!'

Rosa Fierezza saved the file she was working on and closed her laptop. 'Coming,' she yelled, uncurling from the sofa in her bedroom.

But her flatmate was already at her door. She handed her the telephone, and murmured with a wicked grin, 'Some guy with a gorgeous voice and a very sexy, barely there accent? From Niroli, I assume…'

Panic iced through Rosa. New Zealand was half a world away from the island kingdom where she'd been born, youngest in the family of the heir to the throne, and although her sister and brothers kept in close contact, it was always by email except on her birthday.

Her throat closed at the memory of her parents, lost with an uncle in a yachting accident. Swallowing hard, she forced down the fear and said as crisply as she could, 'Hello.'

'Rosa?'

Only two syllables, yet she knew instantly who owned that deep voice, its cool deliberation never quite concealing the undertone of controlled sexuality. Rosa froze, closing her eyes to block out more memories. Her heart contracted painfully, then started racing in wild, impossible hope.

In a quiet, flat tone she said, 'Max? Is it Max?'

'It is, little cousin.' He sounded grave. 'How are you?'

'Fine,' she responded unevenly, also speaking her native language. 'Max, is something wrong?'

He was quick to reassure her. 'Nothing to do with the family. As far as I know everyone is very well.'

Warmth stole back into her skin. The sudden, unbelievable deaths of her parents and uncle had jolted her confidence, making her too conscious of the fragility of life.

Max went on, 'Except Grandpapa, of course, but he's as fit as can be expected for a man of ninety.'

The King of Niroli, their mutual grandfather, was preparing to abdicate after securing the succession. Max had been born so far down the royal line he could never have expected to achieve the throne, until Rosa's brothers and his had scandalously chosen love over their heritage. Now he was the heir.

Rosa asked warily, 'So why have you rung?'

'Because you're the family scientist. Giovanni Carini—do you remember him?—tells me that as part of your master's degree you're researching methods of dealing with shot blight in grapevines.'

'Of course I remember Giovanni.' She smiled as she recalled the elderly man whose whole life had been spent tending the precious vines of Niroli. Then realising what Max had said she drew in a sharp breath. 'Surely not—not shot blight on *Niroli*?'

'Yes.'

She said sharply, 'How much? And where?'

'In at least three vineyards in the Cattina Valley.' His voice was grim.

The icy patch under Rosa's ribs expanded. The valley and the foothills of the mountain range that bisected the island were Niroli's richest vine-growing area, where the famous white grapes of the island flourished.

An epidemic of blight there would be disastrous for the economy.

Quickly she asked, 'Have you quarantined the vineyards?'

'Of course. But I need to know the latest and best way to deal with the outbreak. Can you help?'

A princess of Niroli, Rosa's personal feelings meant nothing compared to the welfare of the people. Shot blight—a vicious disease that first peppered the leaves with holes, then crept inexorably through each vine, eventually killing it— could destroy the ancient vineyards, made immensely valuable over the past years by Max's hard work and brilliant business acumen.

And with the vineyards would die a way of life and a wine that had lasted for over two thousand years. It didn't bear thinking about.

'I hope so,' she said cautiously, wishing she could be more confident. 'We've been working on a method of control that doesn't involve uprooting and burning every vine in a five-kilometre circle around each infected vineyard. It's early days yet, but, if I can get the powers-that-be here to release the spray, we could use this outbreak as a field test.'

'I already have names and contact numbers,' Max said with the steely authority that had always intimidated her. 'They'll release it.'

A wry smile curved Rosa's full lips. If anyone could manage that, Max could.

Years before he'd inherited vineyards in the Cattina Valley, where the region's peasant wine-makers and makers still clung to the methods of the Romans who'd planted the first white grapes on the sunny slopes of the foot-hills. Very little was exported; they'd lived a bare, subsistence life.

Max had changed all that. With Giovanni Carini's aid, and driven by the iron-clad sense of duty that would take him to the throne, he'd used his personal charisma—a formidable blend of authority, inherited charm and intimidating in-telligence—to persuade the growers to join a co-operative that combined the best of their traditional methods with modern wine-making techniques.

The results had been amazing; Porto Castellante Blanco, the wine produced from the area, sold at premium prices all over the world, and the vineyard owners had more security than they'd ever dreamed of—security that could be stolen from them overnight by shot blight.

She had to do what she could to help her fellow countrymen.

In a level, slightly cool voice she said, 'You don't think it would be better if I contacted my superiors instead of you?' Irony infused her final words. 'This is my speciality, and they know me.'

'And I'm sure they are your best friends,' he said, his tone hardening, 'but I have power, and influence, and I'm prepared to use it.'

It sounded arrogant, until he went on, 'The future of Niroli's vineyards—and of thousands of people—depends on getting this outbreak under control. It's the age of the vines that make the wine so magnificent. If we have to uproot them and plant new ones, we'll lose that superb flavour for possibly a whole generation. And that's not taking into account the ten years before we dare plant again.'

Rosa bit her lip. She knew that tone; Max had made up his mind.

What he hadn't said was clear, too. He didn't take her seriously; to him she'd always be the geeky adolescent kid who'd embarrassed him with a passionate crush five years previously.

Not that he'd shown any response to her awkward infatuation, but his previous casual affection had become more studied, more formal, and she'd sensed the wall of reserve behind his friendly attitude.

And a girlfriend—gorgeous, clever and hatefully kind—had appeared within days of Rosa's first blush.

A turbulent mixture of rebellion and remembered pain stiffened her spine. Coolly she said, 'Then all I can do is wish you good luck.'

He said, 'I want you back here. You can speak the language; the vine-growers know you. They'll be more prepared to listen to someone they trust.'

Without giving herself time to react to his words, Rosa said crisply, 'I'll organise that.'

Embarrassed, she realised that her voice held a note of defiance; she controlled it to finish, 'I doubt if even your power and influence will get the spray released without my supervision, and they'll want reports on progress.'

He said levelly, 'I expected no less. Thank you,

little cousin. At this moment the Niroli wine industry needs all the help it can get.'

Rosa had to stop herself from throwing the phone across the room. 'Little cousin'. Two simple words, but with them his reminder that according to the ancient rules of Niroli cousins could not marry. It hadn't been necessary. She was an adult now, and the memory of that humiliating crush was nothing more than a small embarrassment.

So she bade Max an ultra-polite farewell, and waited until the connection was cut before muttering an oath that would have singed his ears.

Then she did five minutes of breathing exercises before washing her face and braving her flatmate's curiosity.

Kate met her at the kitchen door, a mug of coffee in each hand. Thrusting one at Rosa, she asked, 'OK, which cousin was that?'

'Max,' Rosa told her cheerfully, accepting the mug. 'He's the youngest son of my father's younger brother.'

'Oho, the next king!' After a sharp glance at her Kate said, 'Is he as gorgeous as his voice?'

A solicitor, Kate was utterly discreet. During

the media turmoil over the succession to the Niroli throne she'd been frequently ambushed by journalists, only to say brightly each time, 'Sorry, I don't know anything about it.'

To a particularly annoying and persistent member of the foreign press she'd added kindly, 'New Zealanders don't worry about that sort of thing, you know. We take people as they come.'

So Rosa had no hesitation in saying, 'Every bit as gorgeous.'

'Will he make a good king?' Kate enquired.

Rosa said briskly, 'An excellent one. He's an interesting mixture of wine-maker and brilliant, ruthless businessman, but he's big on honour and conscience and responsibility.'

'In other words, he'll hate it,' Kate said shrewdly. 'You know, your dinky island kingdom should really give up this royal thing. OK, the trappings are fabulous, but it seems to be a bar to any sort of happiness. Your brothers and cousins certainly think so—they've all skipped. And your sister has made sure she's never going to be asked to sit on the throne by marrying her rebel tycoon.'

Rosa shrugged. 'It was his father who was the rebel, not Domenic, and Isabella is head over heels in love with him! Anyway, women don't inherit on Niroli.'

'Why not?' In spite of her lack of respect for the institution of monarchy, Kate fired up at this injustice. 'That's outrageous! Don't tell me it's illegal to have a queen!'

'As far as I know there's no actual rule against it.' Rosa frowned. 'Which is interesting, now I think of it. Heaven knows we've got enough other family rules—it's a wonder someone didn't turn that one into law! But I suppose there's always been enough sons to make it unnecessary. However, Max rang to tell me that what seems ominously like shot blight has turned up in Niroli.'

Kate understood enough of Rosa's research to give a low whistle. 'Bad news.' After a glance at Kate's face, she amended that. 'Bad, *bad* news.'

'Very. I'm going home as soon as I can get a flight.'

Instantly Kate said, 'I can do that—I love buying air tickets. The sooner the better? First class all the way?'

'I don't care—if that's the only way to get there, yes.'

'Ah, what it is to be a rich princess,' Kate said

happily, and settled in to make deals, her favourite thing in the world.

'Business class,' she announced triumphantly half an hour later as Rosa locked her suitcase. 'Straight through to Rome, followed by a feeder flight to Porto di Castellante. I'll drive you to the airport.'

Rosa's grateful smile was interrupted by the irritating warble of the telephone.

'Finish organising yourself,' Kate commanded. 'I'll answer it.' She called out a few seconds later, 'It's for you.'

Max again? Rosa swallowed, furious at the thudding of her pulse.

But it was her superior, who she'd rung and failed to get. 'I hear you're leaving us temporarily,' he said drily. 'Your cousin certainly has a way with him—and terrific connections. I've just got an order from God himself to give you and Prince Max every assistance.'

Although he'd probably been startled by the order from above, he sounded intrigued rather than angry. Stifling a sigh of relief, Rosa told him of the situation and together they mapped out a plan of attack.

After she'd hung up she gave a cynical little smile.

Max was renowned for getting his own way. Of course God—known to the world as the CEO of the huge multinational company that owned the lab—had agreed to Max's request. It wasn't every day a future king called for help.

From his vantage point above the concourse, Max scanned Niroli's only international airport, his eyes searching the crowd of tourists. If Rosa had let him take care of the arrangements she'd have flown home on the royal family's private jet, but when his PA rang his cousin with instructions, she'd discovered that Rosa was already on her way.

The door into the room opened to reveal the airport manager, his face wreathed with smiles. 'Your Highness,' he said with a flourish, 'Princess Rosa has arrived.'

Astonished, Max stared at the woman coming towards him. He'd last seen her two years ago at the state funeral of her parents and his father; heavily veiled and clad in deepest mourning, she'd been a tragic figure.

Not so the woman who thanked the manager, waiting until he'd closed the door behind him before turning towards Max with head held high, a slight smile curling lips that were glossed and full, her exotic, tilted eyes enigmatic beneath sleepy lashes. Blue-black hair was caught up in a kind of loose bun, showing off a slender neck and excellent carriage as well as the features that proclaimed her Mediterranean heritage.

Even after a flight from the other side of the world she looked immaculate, long, elegant legs clad in jeans she managed to make both sexy and chic, and her casual, crisp white shirt revealing some very interesting curves...

Although she didn't possess her sister Isabella's glamour and sophistication, she packed a powerful punch. With an effort, Max hauled his thoughts—and his body—back under control.

'Rosa,' he said, smiling.

'Hello, Max.' Her voice revealed a disconcertingly husky note that backed up the unconscious promise of those darkly mysterious eyes.

Angrily Max fought back a surge of reckless desire. Hell and damnation, she was his *cousin*!

Forbidden fruit in every way.

'Welcome to Niroli.' Normally he'd have dropped a brief kiss on both cheeks, but he rapidly discarded that idea.

'I wish it could have been under better circumstances.' She held out a hand in greeting. 'You're looking remarkably cheerful for someone who's fighting blight.'

'And you're looking remarkably bright for someone who's just travelled halfway around the world!' Her fingers were warm, her grip strong—and he responded far too eagerly to her touch.

'I slept on the plane.' Colour tingeing the skin above her sculpted cheekbones, she pulled her hand away.

Startled and irritated by his swift, dangerous reaction, Max asked formally, 'You've come through Customs and Immigration?'

Her amused grin crinkled her eyes. 'If you could call it coming through. All it took was one swift glance at the passport with the crown emblazoned all over it, and the customs officer waved my bag through unopened. Yes, I'm legally on Niroli. Has the stuff from the lab arrived?'

'It came in by freight plane first thing this morning, and is already at Cattina.' He held open the door for her, and once outside said, 'We're driving there straight away—Grandpapa isn't feeling particularly well and his doctors have advised no excitement, so he's sent you his love and his profound gratitude for your help. He'll see you when he's feeling better.'

Were her ears playing tricks, or had he emphasised the word *Grandpapa*—and therefore her close relationship to Max? Yes. Firming her lips, she hid the heat in her skin by nodding so that a wavy lock of black hair fell across her cheek.

On their way down in the elevator she said, 'How ill is he?' When he hesitated, a chilly foreboding scudded the length of her spine. 'You can tell me.'

Max's arrogant jaw tightened. 'He's old and tired and stressed beyond belief by everything that's happened recently, but his doctors are not alarmed by his condition. When he's feeling better I'll bring you back to see him.'

He ushered her out into the sun, still hot and golden and summery.

Rosa glanced up at him, and a fierce, urgent

hunger took her by surprise. He was breathtak-
ingly handsome. Lazy sunlight streaked his
bronze hair, and gilded his angular, tanned face.

Those old genes still held their potency, she
thought, fighting to control her reckless
response. When she'd been five her father had
taken her to see a statue over two thousand years
old, recently excavated in the northern part of
Niroli. The magnificent Grecian-style athlete
with its ancient eyes and dramatic naked beauty
had made a considerable impression on her.

Those same classical features lived again in
Max—and the same hard determination.

He'd make an excellent king, she thought
loyally, and it didn't matter a bit that his ascen-
sion to the throne would finally kill the stupid,
romantic dreams she'd never quite been able to
banish. One of the ancient laws that bound the
ruler of the island kingdom was that he couldn't
marry a blood relation.

When Max had been accepted as the royal heir
she'd accepted that this silly hangover from her
adolescence was doomed.

Unfortunately, it had only taken one glance at
him to demonstrate that she hadn't convinced

some foolish, hidden part of her. When he'd smiled at her that crazy, irrational mixture of anticipation and awareness had sprung into life again like wildfire—dangerous, beautiful, almost uncontrollable.

Well, she had to control it.

'How do you feel about being next in line of succession?' she said as they headed towards an unmarked black car waiting for them in a secure area.

No sooner had the words been spoken than she wished she could call them back. Max's compelling magnetism made him hugely attractive, but he'd always been an intensely private man.

Sure enough, he lifted a dismissive black brow. 'If it has to happen, it has to happen.' His aloof tone indicated she'd stepped over the mark.

Well, she was no longer that lovesick adolescent, shattered when he frowned. 'You'll make an excellent ruler,' she said in a voice that matched his for calm detachment.

A measuring glance from crystalline, green-gold eyes set her heart beating faster, but he made no comment, merely saying as they reached the car, 'Normally I'd have brought the chopper, but it's busy flying the valley.'

Instantly she concentrated on why she was there. Feeling slightly sick, she demanded, 'Another outbreak?'

'Possibly.' After a second he amended that to 'Probably,' and nodded at the man who guarded her luggage. 'Thank you. I'll deal with this now.'

Covertly Rosa watched him open the boot. Powerful muscles in his shoulders rippled beneath the fine cotton of his shirt as he loaded her bag and straightened up. Something stabbed her in the heart. Such blatant male strength drove everything from her mind except an urgent, elemental appreciation.

He caught her looking, and gave her a smile that didn't reach his eyes. 'Let's go,' he said, his detached tone establishing an unbridgeable distance between them. 'We have an industry to save.'

Furious with herself, she slid into the front seat and turned her head to gaze through the side window until she could say sedately, 'I do like the way the new parts of town blend so well with the old.'

'You can thank Grandfather for that,' Max advised, skilfully negotiating the chaos of the city roads. Horns hooted vigorously, and in the donkey-cluttered streets people shouted and sang and gossiped beneath a sky as blue as the sea that surrounded the island. 'He hates what's been done in other Mediterranean cities, so he's kept a tight grip on development here.'

Rosa leaned back and closed her eyes, fighting a stupid sense of rejection. Once more in his face, in his voice, was the barrier he'd erected all those years ago when he'd realised that she was weaving adolescent fantasies, with him as the hero.

Well, this time she'd be as distant, as neutral, as damned controlled as he was.

But it was going to be a long trip to Cattina.

'Rosa.'

The voice, deep and dark and fascinating, wove itself into her dreams. 'Rosa,' it persisted, and she smiled, lifting her lashes to meet cool eyes, their green-gold irises ringed by a tawny rim.

'Max? Where are we?' she asked drowsily, then woke to full alertness. The car had stopped.

His mobile mouth twisted in an ambiguous smile. 'Cattina. Welcome to the real Niroli, little cousin.'

Rosa had had enough. With stiff formality she said, 'Max, I'm no longer a foolish adolescent with a crush on you—I'm a scientist with a job to do.' She tempered her remarks with a slight smile. 'And as I'm an adult and taller than most women, I'm exasperated when you call me little cousin. It sounds like a put-down.'

His smile vanished, and she saw a harder, grimmer Max, his cold green gaze lacking its subtle golden highlights. In a tone that iced across her nerves he stated crisply, 'I'm ten years older than you, so you'll always be my little cousin. Whatever words I use to address you, nothing will ever change that. Accept it, Rosa.'

The cold warning was like a slap in the face, delivered brutally and without emotion. Something inside Rosa—hope?—shrivelled and died, and she hurt so much she couldn't speak.

Hard-won composure came to her rescue. Collecting herself, she shrugged and met his eyes with all the confidence she could summon. 'I suppose those ten extra years—not to mention your new status as heir—give you the right to respect. But if you want the vineyard owners to have confidence in me, you must show it yourself. Calling me *little cousin* in that patronising tone isn't going to do it. When I insist on drastic measures like uprooting whole vineyards, you'll have to back me up, not undermine me by treating me like a child.'

His eyes narrowed and a cynical smile curled his controlled mouth. 'Perhaps I was wrong,' he said after a taut few moments. 'You sound very grown-up. Very well—I'll only call you my little cousin in private.'

He made it sound like a major concession. Gritting her teeth, Rosa forced herself to drag her gaze away from him and look around the courtyard of the castle, a fortress built to protect the pass through the mountains and the river that had made it. In dry, sunny Niroli, water was life.

For centuries the castello had protected this fertile valley from invaders, although some had been successful enough to stamp their mark on the stone walls and battlements.

Hoping she sounded professional and mature, she said, 'I suspect it's going to be difficult to convince the grape-growers that I know what I'm doing. Are they still bound by tradition when it comes to the status of women?'

No, she sounded neither professional nor mature, she thought wearily—just stilted and absurdly formal.

Her cousin looked straight ahead, his angular profile a slashing statement against the mellow stone walls. 'The women have never been as subservient as they seemed, and your sister has changed a lot of ideas about what women can and can't do. Her success with her tourist empire is everyone's pride.'

Isabella had always had spirit and guts and the sheer, dogged determination to succeed. Even though Rosa admired and loved her, Isabella's success made her feel lacking in some vital way.

Warily she watched Max get out and walk around the front of the car. As he was opening her door a manservant came down the steps from the huge doors and efficiently removed her luggage. Rosa climbed out, wincing at the immediate protest of muscles that had barely been used in the past thirty-six hours.

'Jet-lagged?' Max asked, taking her arm.

Sensation arced through her, swift and daunting and clamorous. Her teeth clenched a moment on her bottom lip and she stared blindly ahead, mounting the steps by guesswork and will power. 'I'm just a bit stiff,' she managed to say brightly. 'It's a long way from New Zealand to Niroli.'

Perhaps he felt that powerful charge too, for he released her. In a steady, almost bland voice he said, 'If you hadn't jumped the gun you could have travelled in much more comfort in the royal plane.' And then, in an entirely different voice, guarded and remote, 'Welcome to my home, Rosa.'

'Thank you,' she said automatically, walking beside him into the cool dimness of the great hall.

CHAPTER TWO

ISABELLA had raved about Max's conversion of
the castle's rugged austerity into a habitation that
combined the authority of the past with modern
luxury. But before Rosa had time to notice much
more than a splendid—and probably priceless—
Oriental rug and a huge Renaissance coffer, a
massive yawn split her face.

Oh, how adult and sophisticated! she thought
in mortification, hastily covering it with her hand.

Max looked amused. 'Poor little one—you
must be exhausted. I'll take you to your room, and
I suggest you have a small snack and then sleep.'

'I certainly won't say no to something to eat.'
Rosa salvaged what poise she could and smiled
at the manservant.

'What would you like?' Max asked.

'Food from the island?' she suggested. 'Just
olives and a salad, with coffee?'

One glance from Max sent the beaming man-servant on his way.

She said firmly, 'Then I'll wash the journey away, and after that I want to see the vineyards that are under quarantine.'

Max indicated the staircase that swept up ahead of them. They were halfway up the flight when he said silkily, 'Proving something, Rosa?'

'Possibly,' she returned, meeting his sardonic gaze directly. Her stomach clamped and a shiver of response whispered the length of her spine, but she needed to establish her competence in this. 'I'm sure you know that time is of the essence when it comes to dealing with shot blight. I need to have those vines—and the lab results too.'

'You look tired. You'll be better able to make sense of things when you've had a proper night's sleep.'

'I can cope,' she said, utterly determined that she should prove herself to be—what? Competent? Independent? Knowledgeable?

All of those, and then some. If she were Isabella he wouldn't be treating her like a fractious ten-year-old.

Max's shoulders lifted a fraction. 'Of course,' he said smoothly. 'I wasn't implying that you couldn't.'

He delivered her to the door of her room, told her that he'd see her soon, and left. Once inside she stood a moment, letting her eyes roam while her heartbeat settled back into its normal pace.

A difficult mixture of exhilaration and caution blended into apprehension. She'd been so sure she was over him, and she'd been so wrong. Oh, she no longer assumed that her response was love—she'd learned something in the years since she'd been sixteen! This was lust, simple, un-complicated animal attraction; the turbulent, rather degrading flash-fire reaction that set hormones surging in mindless hunger.

OK, so her wretched body seemed compelled to goad her into heady awareness whenever he came near her, but at least she'd shown him that her mind was her own. She bit her lip and headed for the bathroom.

Spending the rest of her life longing for a man she could never have wasn't an option. Especially, she thought wryly, when it was obvious that he still saw her as the kid who'd embarrassed him with her unruly emotions five years ago.

She splashed cold water over her face, and stood a moment, staring at herself in the mirror. The *en suite* was cool and luxurious yet spare, almost austere, befitting a castle that had seen Saracens and Crusaders and various other marauders come and go.

Pride insisted that Max accept her as a responsible adult. If she achieved that she'd go back to New Zealand with the knowledge not only of a job well done—she hoped—but of her own progress from girlish infatuation to adult autonomy.

'You sound like a self-help book,' she scoffed beneath her breath. 'Clearly you need a cold shower to clear your brain.'

Refreshed by the play of cool water on her skin, Rosa wrapped herself in a towel and strolled into the bedroom to discover a maid unpacking her clothes and transferring them into a walk-in wardrobe. They exchanged smiling greetings before Rosa chose a simple cotton dress to wear.

She was frowning at her reflection when a knock on the door brought the food she'd asked for.

Perhaps she should try for a more professional image instead of this informal comfort? After all, she needed to look reliable and competent.

And as she was going to be walking around vineyards, it had to be practical.

A swift examination of her wardrobe revealed casual cotton trousers and a shirt in a paler shade of olive. A loose scarf in olive and copper and dark blue would protect her neck from the sun, still bold and burning in late summer. She changed, and pulled on a pair of ankle-height leather boots, frowning when she imagined what several dowsings in antiseptic troughs would do to them.

'Memo—buy gumboots,' she said ironically into the silent room.

Satisfied, she sat down to eat at the table set in the narrow window. It was poignant to be here relishing the tastes of Niroli without her parents or her sister. She blinked back a swift ache of tears for the dead, and concentrated on Isabella, happily enjoying life with the new husband who adored her.

Her grief subsided slowly as she enjoyed the crisp salad with local green olives and olive oil, and the hard, tasty cheese made only on the island from the milk of the ewes pastured high in the mountains.

'How was your lunch?' Max asked as he drove her to the first vineyard, navigating narrow twisty lanes with the familiarity of long acquaintance.

'Delicious,' she said on a sigh. 'New Zealand has the best food in the world, but it's impossible to achieve the exact flavours of Niroli there. Even their herbs taste subtly different.'

'What do you think of New Zealand?'

Because it was a safe, neutral subject, she enlarged on her experiences in the small South Pacific country. 'It's—wild,' she finished, her mind seeing again a range of mountains rising above plains, the thick rainforest of the north with its massive trees, and perfect beaches set like melon slices against a sea as green as emeralds that stretched for infinity. 'Here everything bears the mark of mankind; there, vast areas are untouched and pristine. And there are so few people—well, except for the cities, of course. But even they're small.'

He nodded. 'I've been there.'

Startled, she looked at him. When? Had it been

while she was there? And because she couldn't ask him, she said in a neutral voice, 'What did *you* think of it?'

'Like you, I loved the wildness.' He grinned suddenly. 'And although it was five years ago, before things really got going with their wine industry, I liked what I saw—and drank—of their wine.'

Some stupid part of Rosa was relieved that he hadn't come to New Zealand and ignored her.

He went on thoughtfully, 'I envied them the opportunity to build a whole industry from scratch, to take it to the world.'

Intrigued, Rosa pointed out, 'But that's what you've done here.'

His wide shoulders lifted. 'Perhaps,' he conceded. 'But the grapes and the knowledge were already here—the local conditions were as familiar to the growers as their own wives' faces. It was a matter of modernisation rather than innovation, and of course I had help.'

She sent him a curious glance.

Answering her unspoken question, he said, 'Giovanni could see the need for progress, and because he'd made such a success of the royal vineyards he has great prestige amongst the peasants. If it hadn't been for his support it would have been a much harder fight.'

Rosa nodded. She was learning things about him, small, precious nuggets of information to be hoarded away in the deepest recesses of her brain like stolen gems.

'Even without Giovanni you'd have won them around,' she said drily. 'Failure doesn't seem to be a word you accept.'

'It happens,' he said, an aloof note in his voice slamming barriers against her. 'Here's the first vineyard.'

Two soldiers with rifles manned the barricade across the road that led to the afflicted vineyards. When they realised who was driving the car they sprang to attention and saluted, then drew back the bar so the car could make its way through a wide shallow bath of disinfectant.

'No entrance without a permit,' Max said briefly. 'So far the precautions seem to be working. The vines were pruned immediately and every leaf and twig burnt.' He glanced at her intent face. 'I hope to God we can save them.'

'So do I,' she said quietly. 'But it's not likely—once the blight gets into the plants, they're doomed and have to be burnt, roots and all. The best we can hope for is to stop the infection from spreading beyond the immediate vicinity.'

'How?' His voice was almost aggressive. 'It's devastated every other area it's struck.'

'We've developed an antibiotic that might turn the tide. It's carefully targeted to the bacterium that causes shot blight, so it won't kill every other good thing in the soil. But even if it works, it won't save infected vines; what we're hoping is that it will stop the spread of the disease for long enough to contain it.'

'So the vineyards that are affected will still be destroyed.'

'I'm afraid so,' she admitted quietly. 'But if we drench the soil between them and their neighbours, we might save the others.'

Giovanni was waiting for them with a small group in the walled courtyard between the house and the road. Rosa smiled at him as the car stopped, wondering at the odd flash of recognition that teased her brain. The years might have wrinkled his face, but nothing could hide its magnificent framework. In his youth he must have been gorgeous.

Those Mediterranean genes, she thought wryly, had a lot to answer for.

Getting out of the car, she stood too quickly and stumbled. To an instant outcry, she grabbed the car door and clung to the hot metal, willing her legs to straighten and her head to remain erect.

Max got to her before anyone else. Strong arms closed around her and she was held against his lean body, her face pressed into his chest.

'You should damned well have gone to bed, you silly little idiot!' Above her whirling head he directed a stream of orders to the waiting family, orders that resounded in Rosa's ears with all of the meaning of distant thunder.

But she heard enough to say faintly, 'I'm perfectly all right! I mean it, Max! I am not going to lie down.'

Apart from the brief handshake at the airport, it was the first time he'd touched her. At sixteen she'd woven dreams around him, obsessively read newspapers that detailed his conquests, and wept in secret because she'd known she was never going to look like his elegant lovers.

But she'd always known she could never be close to him. So although the heat of his body was a potent lure now, summoning rivulets of fire in her bloodstream, she managed to stiffen and pull herself away, using stubborn will-power to hold her head high.

'Are you all right?' he demanded, inspecting her narrowed eyes, his voice rough with anger. And something else.

Men could feel passion for any woman; love wasn't necessary. But even as she saw him reimpose the control that rejected her, some secret, wicked part of Rosa rejoiced at the arousal she'd felt in his body, the swift, heated response he hadn't been able to hide.

She drew in a deep breath and smiled mistily at the concerned family and Giovanni. 'Jet lag,' she said succinctly. 'I'm so sorry for startling you like that.'

The owner of the vineyard turned to his wife and barked, 'Mirella, woman, what are you thinking? Don't stand there—get the princess a glass of wine.'

'No, no, I'd rather have water,' Rosa said hastily.

The water was already on its way, handed over by the daughter of the house.

Rosa drained the glass, then said, 'Ah, that's much better! Now I feel myself again.'

But as they tramped the vines she was uneasily aware of Max's scrutiny. He was rarely more than a step away from her until they went back to the house, where they were fortified by magnificent coffee and a slice of blackberry tart served by the women of the house.

The owner asked gruffly, 'So, what is the verdict, Highness?'

'I won't know for certain until I see the lab results,' she told him, wishing she could reassure him. 'But I'm afraid it doesn't look like good news.'

There was collective silence, broken when the owner crossed himself and said bleakly, 'It is in God's hands. Thank you for coming to help us.'

Rosa blinked back tears after they left, this time with Giovanni in the back seat of the car.

Max asked with cold abruptness, 'Are you all right?'

Aware of the elderly man behind them, Rosa said briskly, 'Yes, I'm fine, thank you. I still feel silly, staggering like a drunk when I got out of the car; it *was* just jet lag, along with muscles that need to be used.'

She directed a smile over her shoulder, somewhat surprised when she met the older man's solemn, dark gaze.

Formally he said, 'It would perhaps be a good idea to take you back to the castello so that you can sleep.'

'I need to accustom myself to Niroli time,' she told him. 'And I want to see all three affected vineyards.'

Max said coolly, 'She is no longer the sweet child we once knew, Giovanni.'

'Life goes on,' Giovanni replied. 'People change, but some things always stay the same. Family and the good earth are all we can rely on. And God, of course.'

Rosa had been admiring the hills, their slopes braided with vines, but she risked a glance at Max's profile—aloof and aristocratic against the golden light outside. It could have been her imagination, but she thought his mouth had compressed.

Perhaps Giovanni had merely succumbed to one of the privileges of age—making sententious statements—but his words had sounded perilously close to a warning.

Her head lifted and she squared her shoulders. Yes, Giovanni had been on the royal island the summer she was sixteen, supervising the harvest. No doubt he too recalled her hopeless crush.

If it's the last thing I do, she vowed savagely, I'm going to show everyone who remembers that stupid, futile infatuation that I'm well and truly over it!

Max said, 'Why are these vines affected, yet not the ones in the adjacent vineyards?'

Relieved, she turned her attention back to the problems of shot blight. 'We don't know, but it can start like this, in scattered areas rather than clusters.'

'So every vineyard in the valley will have to be constantly monitored.'

'Exactly.'

Silence fell as they contemplated the enormous task this would be.

Rosa said quietly, 'Another problem is that methods of control that show promise in one part of the world often don't work in another. It's fascinating, because so far it hasn't followed any pattern, yet there must be one.'

'There speaks the scientist.' Max's tone was dry. 'You see an intriguing problem—I see people whose livelihoods and lives are at huge risk.'

Hurt, she returned, 'I don't forget them.'

Ahead of them the white road narrowed into a farm track; another barricade and two more soldiers prevented entry. Again the soldiers snapped to attention and saluted, then swung the barrier back to let the car through the bath of solution.

It was a process repeated several hours later at the last of the three vineyards. Similar too, were the anxious faces of those who depended on the grapes, their heavy, palpable fear wringing Rosa's heart.

At the final one an aged patriarch, brown and seamed by the sun, told her, 'Highness, we are praying you can help us.'

'I will do my best,' she said, miserably conscious of just how futile that promise might be.

Stooped but vigorous after a lifetime spent tending the vines, his wife demanded sharply, 'What will happen if you cannot?'

Rosa met her worried gaze and hesitated. It hurt her to say the words, but false promises would only make things worse.

While she was choosing the least blunt way to say it, Max said harshly, 'The truth.'

Rosa repressed a swift spurt of anger. She understood how he felt; the improved wines of Cattina were his creation. To a man as strong and powerful as he was, defeat would be especially bitter. 'The vines will have to be uprooted and burnt, and the land kept free of them for at least ten years.'

The woman wailed, striking her hand to her forehead then covering her mouth while she rocked back and forth, her faded eyes staring into some bleak future.

Max said crisply, 'It may not come to pass; if it does, that is the time to weep. But whatever happens, you will not starve. I will see to that.'

The old man hushed his wife. With a slight bow to Max, he said, 'And we will thank you for that, Highness, even those of us who fought your scheme. But these vines are older than my grandfather; I know them as well as I know my grandchildren. Besides, new plantings will produce only thin, poor wine for at least another generation. If this blight kills the island's vines, not even you will be able to save our wine.'

Max said decisively, 'Then we will learn to produce good wines from the young grapes.'

It was commonly accepted that the vines produced no wine worth drinking until they were at least fifty years old, but if anyone could work a miracle it would be Max.

On the way back to the castle, Rosa commented, 'From what you just said, I gather you've got some sort of social welfare scheme going here.'

'Yes,' Max said briefly.

From behind Giovanni interposed, 'He fought the king long and hard for this, and fought the vine-growers even longer and harder, but they are grateful now.'

'Silence, old man,' Max said, but without heat. He negotiated a flock of sheep heading for the hills. 'At first my grandfather could see no necessity for such a scheme, and neither could the growers. They are fiercely independent, but they came around in the end, thanks to Giovanni.'

The old man chuckled. 'You do me too much

honour—it was your authority and logic that won over the stubborn king and the even more stubborn vineyard owners. Also, you promised that the co-operative would match their contributions—and that you would underwrite the scheme until it was viable.'

Impressed, and oddly proud, Rosa said, 'That's wonderful.'

Max shrugged. 'They're hard bargainers.'

Giovanni said, 'They do not have to wring every penny from their grapes now just to survive. They can afford to plan, to improve, to use the land wisely.' After a moment he added, 'But if this outbreak is not confined, all that will go.'

A heavy weight of responsibility weighed Rosa down. It must be even worse for Max. 'I need to check the lab results,' she said, smothering a yawn that came out of nowhere.

From behind Giovanni objected gruffly, 'Highness, you sent us medicines for the vines. Should we not use them immediately?'

'No,' she said, gently but firmly. 'It's still experimental, and there simply isn't enough of it to waste. I must be sure that it's shot blight.'

Max smiled in irony. 'It's strange for us who remember Rosa as a young filly, all arms and legs and a mane of hair in her eyes, to see her as an expert, but she is. So we do what she says.'

He sounded like an uncle—no, a great-uncle! Disinterested, detached and withdrawn.

'Thank you,' she said tonelessly, fighting back a betraying edge of frustration. 'I'll do the best I can, but I can't make any promises about success.'

Max turned the car into the castle forecourt. 'The only alternative is to watch the entire industry shrivel and die.'

He pulled up at the bottom of the steps that led to the two huge doors into the great hall. 'Come inside for a drink,' he said to Giovanni.

'If you're going to discuss anything, I need to be there,' Rosa said tightly.

'What use would you be now?' he asked in open irony as she hid another yawn. 'What you need is at least twelve hours sleep.'

'I'm perfectly all—'

'You are not!' he said, cutting her off with formidable authority. 'Your eyes are smudged and you can't stop yawning. Go to bed now and sleep the night away, and tomorrow you'll be able to give your full attention to this problem.'

He was right, damn him! Clinging to her composure, she turned to Giovanni. 'It's been lovely to see you again,' she said with a smile. 'I just wish it had been on some more auspicious occasion.'

The old man nodded, his expression solemn. 'Your servant, Highness,' he said formally.

Clearly his faith in her power to halt the epidemic was pretty minimal. As, she suspected, was Max's. His decision to call her across the world had been one of desperation, made only because he had no other recourse.

After showering again, she transcribed the comments she'd made from the recorder to the laptop, then ate about half the dinner brought up to her. She tried to assess the lab tests, but even two cups of coffee couldn't keep her awake. Within about two minutes the words started dancing in front of her and she had to put the papers down and crawl into bed, surrendering to sleep.

Some time during the night she woke, climbed groggily out to get a glass of water, and stood at the window to drink it. The town that clustered around the castle was dark except for the few streetlights, fading now. Morning had to be on the way, although no dawn-glow lightened the eastern sky. Rosa felt as though she'd slept too long and too heavily—slightly headachy, her bones still heavy, her eyes gritty.

She picked up the papers that held the lab tests, but put them down again without looking at them, and crept back into the huge bed, to lie watching the stars in the dark sky.

She'd been so sure that whatever she'd felt for Max had been conquered, a victim of the years and her maturity. Perhaps she should have guessed that it had merely gone underground; after all, there had been no other man for her. At twenty-one she was still a virgin. Bleakly, and for the first time, she faced the fact that no other man had ever meant anything because Max still filled her mind and her heart. Oh, she'd had mild flings, but the instant anything looked like getting serious she'd backed off.

More worryingly, the childish puppy love of her teens had transmuted into something much more dangerous—a driving hunger that shook her to the core whenever he was near. His voice—deep, dark and distinctive—sent shivers of pleasure through her.

And when he'd held her…

Angrily she tried to dismiss the memories, but they persisted, new-minted and sharp as though hours hadn't passed. In his arms she'd felt completely and utterly safe—except from her own needs and hunger.

And when she'd rested for a moment against his big, lean body, it had hardened against her, and for a second she'd understood the power of sexuality. That moment of recognition, of revelation, had melted her bones. Making love to Max would be heaven.

Ruthlessly she refused to let her mind travel down that banned path. In other parts of the world cousins could marry, but not if you belonged to the royal family of Niroli.

A humourless smile creased her lips as she remembered Kate's shock when she'd heard about that arcane set of strictures put into place by Rosa's ancestors for reasons that had probably seemed excellent at the time.

'Outrageous!' she'd exclaimed. 'And does *everyone* have to obey them?'

'No, just everyone in the royal family.'

Incredulously Kate said, 'So once you get to be King you can think up whatever weird law you want and everyone has to obey or be expelled from the royal family? That's simply asking for trouble. What if you get a crazy king?'

'The rules were all made up centuries ago and no ruler can add to them—or at least, not as far as I know. And you're not thrown out of the family if you do disobey one—you just can't be King.'

'Pity you're not in line to succeed,' Kate said pithily. 'You could have done something about hauling that backward little place into the nineteenth century.'

'It's not that bad,' Rosa protested, but Kate had shaken her head and gone off muttering.

In the huge bed, Rosa sighed and closed her eyes…

It was broad daylight when she woke again. Sunlight had threaded its way through the gap she'd left in the heavy drapes, falling in shafts across the ancient Oriental carpet so that the room glowed with a soft mellow light.

Someone had arranged vases of flowers

around the room; they glowed like miniature suns, their shaggy heads concentrating all the tawny colours of late summer. She was wondering if Max had thought about it, when a gentle tap on the door brought her upright.

'Come in,' she called, her heart thumping unevenly.

CHAPTER THREE

OF COURSE it wasn't Max! Instead a maid brought in a tray. On it, to Rosa's wistful delight, was the simple breakfast of her childhood, thick yoghurt with honey, chewy peasant bread and olive oil and fruit—oranges and figs and a handful of pistachio nuts.

And coffee…

Eyes half closed, Rosa inhaled the scent of it, rich and redolent and so typical of Niroli, and broke into a broad smile. 'Now I know I'm home!' she exclaimed.

With a wide, pleased grin the maid curtsied and left her.

It was a comment Max repeated as they walked through the streets to the scientific complex he'd set up to help the growers with their problems. 'Irene—the maid—told me that it was the coffee that made you feel at home,' he said. 'I'm surprised. From what I remember New Zealand has excellent coffee.'

'Oh, yes, but it's not made the way it is here. No other coffee anywhere else in the world smells like it.'

'You've been to so many other parts?'

She shrugged. 'A few,' she said, adding, 'Not as many as you, of course.'

'Ah, but I've had ten extra years to travel,' he drawled, and indicated a modern building that paid discreet tribute to the ancient houses around it. 'Here we are.'

Always that reminder, she thought wearily. She banished the ache in her heart with a bright smile as she met the head of the research facility, who welcomed her with a slight air of reserve.

No doubt he thought she was a dilettante. Setting her jaw, Rosa worked hard to remove that impression, and was rewarded when he offered to show her around the installation. It was a relief to walk into a lab that could have been the one in New Zealand, although here again she met that slight, wary resistance.

As though a princess can't be a scientist too, she thought indignantly.

Or perhaps it was her youth that made her suspect. Well, she couldn't help being a nerd! Accelerated learning had meant she'd achieved her university degree two years before most others, but although she'd had to prove herself over and over again, it was always irritating.

This was what Max must have faced when he'd used his ancestral estates to show the local wine-growers that they could produce high-grade wine. He'd been only nineteen when he'd inherited the Cattina Valley estates.

Rosa squared her shoulders. He'd proved himself; so would she. The connection warmed her, easing the worry that hovered at the back of her brain—the fear that she wasn't going to be able to help.

Half an hour of discussion in the lab eased the covert reservations; the researchers soon crowded around, asking questions about the latest progress in New Zealand, and she was immediately immersed in shop-talk.

But not so immersed that she didn't know when Max took his leave—or when he came back. Even before she heard his voice some primitive sense of recognition tightened the skin on the back of her neck so that each tiny hair stood up. It took a considerable effort to keep her mind on the conversation she was having with one of the technicians.

Across the lab, Max fought back a hot, lethally possessive desire to stride across there and yank her away from the young man who was gazing at her with such masked appreciation.

A reckless territorial instinct took over his brain, almost banishing the fact that because she was his cousin he had no right to feel anything other than mild, totally platonic affection for her.

Furious at his weakness, he said in a level, controlled voice, 'We have to go.'

Rosa's head came up; Max judged to a nicety the exact angle of her square, stubborn little chin as she tilted it at him.

Her dark eyes gleamed with exasperation, but before she had a chance to say anything Max asked, 'Unless you need more time here?'

Reluctantly she said, 'Not at the moment. Before I start work I want to ask my boss in New Zealand some questions.' She glanced at her watch. 'But it will be the middle of the night in New Zealand, so I'd better email rather than ring him.'

As they walked back to the castle, he said, 'That can wait until after lunch.'

And after lunch came siesta, Max thought. He increased the speed of his stride, silently cursing the way his body reacted to the busy interference of his hormones, conjuring up tantalising images of long hours spent in a bed with her while the hot sun drowsed across the sky and the island slept…

Ruthlessly he blocked them. It had to be, he decided grimly, a particularly cynical fate with a malicious sense of humour that had transformed his gawky, round-shouldered cousin with her large spectacles and rather touching crush into this elegant, long-legged creature.

Add to that skin like the finest silk sleeked by a drift of gold dust, exotic tilted eyes that held a challenging gleam and a mouth that didn't have to say a word to make promises…

Rosa was trouble. Forbidden trouble.

It had been some months since he'd taken a woman to his bed, but it had been at least ten years since he'd stopped responding to beautiful women with the undisciplined eagerness of a high-school boy.

Now he noted one of the local men eyeing her with the frank appreciation of the islanders, and was transfixed by a pang of savage jealousy that came out of nowhere. That was all he needed in this crisis, he thought cuttingly—a stupid, futile lust for a cousin so young she was barely more than a schoolgirl.

An innocent one, at that. Unless she'd been totally discreet, she was probably still a virgin.

A fierce desire to be the first man in her bed startled him; he'd never demanded to be the first with his lovers. But more shocking—and infinitely more dangerous, he instinctively knew—was the unusual tenderness that underpinned the physical hunger.

Once inside the great hall of the castle he said abruptly, 'I hope you don't mind eating your lunch by yourself. I have work that won't wait.'

Rosa looked up into a face shuttered against her. 'Of course not,' she said automatically. 'I have work to do too. Is the castello hooked up to the internet?'

His smile was sardonic. 'This is Niroli, not the end of the world. Just use the telephone jack.'

Inside her room, Rosa bit her lip. Stupid,

stupid—of course the castle had every conceivable electronic aid for the modern businessman. Max ran a huge investment banking concern from here. Straightening her shoulders, she booted up her laptop and told herself she didn't care if he was moody.

It was stupid to feel that he resented her. He had much more important things to think about than a stray cousin here to do a job before she went back to New Zealand.

Much later, after siesta, she walked down the staircase, admiring the art that adorned it. His taste interested her—along with the requisite old masters, the castello was adorned by an eclectic display of modern art, bold yet strikingly at home on the ancient stone walls.

Smiling at the manservant who appeared as she reached the hall, she said, 'I need coffee and fresh air.'

'This way, Your Highness.' He showed her to a courtyard.

She looked around, delight swelling inside her. Years before, someone had grafted this enchanted place onto the grim old castle, filling it with roses still in flower, their perfume heavy in the warm air. A mellow stone fountain splashed serenely, and grapevines cast a pool of shade on the flags of the wide terrace. In several pots gardenias bloomed, the chaste white flowers at odds with their sultry perfume.

Loungers and chairs and a big wooden table revealed that this part of the castello was well used. She hesitated, but stiffened her spine and walked into the shade.

Her heart jumped when Max came out through a door in a wall of gracious nineteenth-century glass. If he was surprised to see her it didn't show in his handsome face, although his survey of her was keen and too perceptive. 'Sleep well?' he asked.

She hid her sharpened senses with a wry smile. 'It didn't take me long to surrender to old habits. Very well, thank you.'

'Good. Sit down and have a glass of lemonade—or would you prefer coffee?'

'Home-made lemonade?'

'Of course,' he said, brows rising.

'It sounds wonderful. And I'd like some coffee too, please, to chase away the sleep.'

The drinks came accompanied by small cakes

and fresh fruit. Knowing dinner would be later than she was accustomed to, Rosa ate gratefully and caught up on news of the family.

Finally, however, she said, 'I have bad news, I'm afraid.'

His face hardened. 'Tell me,' he commanded.

She took a deep breath. 'My boss in New Zealand agrees that it is shot blight, and so the vines on the three infected vineyards must be removed and burnt. It's too late to save them.'

Muttering something explosive, Max got to his feet in a single, lithe movement. Rosa watched him pace out into the sunlight, the rays burnishing his head into bronze fire, his face set in stern, angry lines.

He stopped and swung around, fixing her with a coldly formidable gaze. 'You're sure of this?'

'I'm sorry, but, yes, we all are—the lab here, the lab at home and me. We're all agreed that the soil in the infected vineyards should be fumigated.' Honesty compelled her to finish, 'But even then there are no guarantees.'

And because she guessed how he must feel, she went across to stand beside him, giving the only support she thought he'd take from her. The cheerful splash and murmur of the fountain faded into the background. 'I'm sorry,' she said again.

'Stop apologising—it's not your fault.'

His aggressive tone hurt, but he wasn't being personal; he had to tell his growers this bad news, and she didn't blame him for being angry with fate or the gods or whatever had sent this blight.

She said, 'Most outbreaks occur during a wet spring and sweep through the area like wildfire; the fact that this arrived in late summer, and is confined to only three vineyards, could be a hopeful sign.'

'It had better be,' he said grimly, and looked down at her, his mouth twisting. 'Very well, the three confirmed vineyards will be razed, every last twig and root burned and the land kept out of grape production for at least ten years.'

'It's the only thing that's worked.'

'I know. What about the adjacent vineyards?'

Rosa swallowed. 'Although there's no sign of the blight in them, I think they should be burned too—as a precaution. If we don't have any more than three other outbreaks we've got enough spray to—with any luck—control it in the valley.'

His lips compressed into a thin, severe line. 'It's not going to be easy to convince the affected growers when their vines show no signs of disease.'

'I know,' Rosa said. 'But they trust you—that's obvious. You might be surprised.'

He frowned. 'It seems I dragged you all this way for nothing.'

Stifling a stab of pain at his bluntness, she returned it. 'I doubt if you'd have got the spray without someone to accompany it to oversee its use.'

He regarded her with lifted brows. 'Really?' he drawled.

'Really,' she returned with spirit. 'Agricultural sprays are big business—the CEO wouldn't have released it unless someone he trusted accompanied it. As well, technicians need to be shown exactly how to monitor the vines, what to look for and how to record the results of the tests they do. And my boss wants full and accurate reports of everything we do.' Pride drove her to finish, 'Once that's all under way, I'll go home.'

'Home? Do you think of New Zealand as home?'

Startled, she paused before saying on a note of surprise, 'I suppose I do—for now, anyway. I love it there, and I feel I'm doing good work. I might even try and do my doctorate over there.'

A dove cooed forlornly in the grapevines. Frowning, Max kept his eyes fixed on the bird while he said with unexpected gentleness, 'Forgive me, Rosa—I'm taking my anger out on you and that's not fair. You've already energised the researchers—the head of the institute told me that his assistants are now eager to get to work on several new lines you suggested.'

'I'm glad,' she said simply. She hesitated before asking, 'Do you want me to tell the growers what has to be done?' Before he could answer she hurried on, 'I don't have to live here; bad news might come easier from me.'

His gaze softened as it rested on her lips, then heated. Colour rose unbidden to her skin. Dry-mouthed, she fought back a powerful surge of sensation that sang through her veins like warm honey, sweeping away inhibitions.

After that hooded, dangerous glance Max

turned away as though the sight of her irritated him. 'Thank you for offering, but I owe it to them to do it.'

Max knew he'd hurt her, but her damned innocence was both challenge and protection. Without realising it, Rosa was too tempting. He wanted nothing more than to kiss the grave concern from her lips, to feel them cling hungrily to his and then to carry her across to a lounger and make her his in every possible way.

In bed the previous night he'd tossed for hours, trying to banish her from his mind so that he could sleep. Yet when he did at last manage to, she'd invaded his dreams, those dark siren's eyes veiled and mysterious, her mouth inviting as she whispered sweet promises to him.

Because she was his cousin, she was completely forbidden.

He'd be the next King of Niroli. For all his grandfather's faults, he loved the old man who worried incessantly about the welfare of his country. There was no one else now to take over; the only other male descendant was illegitimate.

He was *it*, he thought savagely. Born so far

from the throne that he'd never dreamed of having to take up its burden, he'd now accepted it. In a way he'd even looked forward to it. His grandfather ruled autocratically, using the island parliament more as a sounding-board than a governing body. Max had been prepared to sacrifice his privacy and his freedom for Niroli so that he could introduce modern democracy to the island.

Hell, he thought with sudden, cold disgust at himself, he'd been smug. This fierce wildfire passion had the potential to derail his plans.

If he let it.

He'd always prided himself on his self-control, yet one heavy-lidded glance from Rosa's exotic tilted eyes, dark with hidden thoughts, had splintered his defences into matchsticks.

Speaking with surprising passion, she blurted, 'I wish I could be more help. I wish I could tell you we had a cure.'

'Setting up links with the lab here is important, and will probably become more so in the future,' he told her, glad of the interruption. Then, because he wanted other people around them, he suggested, 'Shall we fly to Porto di Castellante tonight and have dinner there?'

Rosa clamped down on a wildfire spurt of delicious anticipation. 'That would be lovely. I haven't visited Grandpapa yet. Can you organise that for me—if he's well enough, of course?'

'I'll see how his doctors feel,' Max told her.

That evening Rosa hauled out the one dress that might do for dinner in the capital. Black silk energised by white polka dots, its scooped neck revealed the soft swell of her breasts. Frowning, she wondered if she was revealing too much golden skin.

Then she shrugged. When she'd arrived in New Zealand she'd been so impressed by Kate's elegance that she'd asked her flatmate to recommend a make-up expert. This woman had not only shown her how to emphasise the natural tilt of her eyes and her sweeping cheekbones, but told her that she should be proud of her assets.

'You've got a fabulous figure—you could be a model if you stood straighter. And your breasts are just right, not too big or too small. But you can certainly wear lower necklines—although not too low, because overtly sexy is not your style. Your skin is just gorgeous.'

Rosa had been startled, but the woman's chic

confidence had made her more than willing to listen. 'I thought of cutting my hair,' she said tentatively.

'Don't you dare! Use it to balance your height. And for heaven's sake, get rid of those flat heels.'

'But I tower over just about everyone,' Rosa explained.

'Who cares? Oh, only short men with inferiority complexes, that's who! Why worry about them? You've got the most elegant pair of ankles I've seen for years, and legs that go on for ever. Play to your assets. Show the world that you appreciate yourself. And walk every day for twenty minutes with a book on your head until you've got rid of that stoop.'

Rosa had obeyed, helped by Kate's recommendation of a good gym; also with Kate's help she'd learned what clothes suited her, and she'd developed a style to suit her exotic looks.

For Max, she thought now, pulling out her black sandals, high and elaborately strapped to call attention to those ankles. It had all been for Max.

Even when she'd accepted that she might never see him again, she'd been transforming herself for him.

'Idiot!' she muttered bleakly at her reflection. Common sense told her she was crazy; instead of dressing for Max she should stay at the castle and work out a plan of action for dealing with shot blight.

Common sense could go hang; she was never likely to have the chance to go out with him again. She pinned a tremulous smile to her lips and ran down the staircase.

The helicopter landed at the private pad in the grounds of the royal palace. Rosa's gaze travelled from the royal standard—the family coat of arms emblazoned on the brilliant blue that stood for the sea surrounding Niroli—to the waiting car with its discreet lack of insignia. 'Is there any chance I might be able to see Grandpapa tonight?' she asked.

'I'm afraid not.' In the back seat of the vehicle after the chauffeur had set it in motion, Max explained, 'He's still very tired and his doctors are insisting that he stay in bed without visitors for another couple of days. The yachting tragedy was a huge blow to him; he's never really recovered.'

'It was a huge blow to all of us,' she said in a muted voice.

He slid his hand over hers and gripped for a second. 'To all of us,' he agreed, removing it.

His touch was entirely sexless, and supremely comforting. The whole family had sought comfort together, but that swift clasp of Max's strong hand had eased the last raw spot in her heart. 'And I suppose all this turmoil about the succession had just piled on the agony for Grandpapa.'

'Yes.' His voice was clipped and level. 'He's fragile, and his doctors are careful.'

She risked a glance at his angular profile. 'Do you want to be King?'

Max's mouth hardened. 'It's not a matter of wanting. I have to be King. Put simply, there's no one else left.' After a pause that lasted for just a second too long, he drawled, 'Unless you want to take it on?'

Shuddering, Rosa shook her head so vehemently that a lock of hair fell from her loose chignon. She tucked it back in and said with heartfelt earnestness, 'Apart from the fact that Niroli has never had a woman ruler, I'd hate it.'

'But if it happened you'd accept the responsibility, and do your best.'

The pool of ice beneath her ribs expanded as a cold shiver of foreboding ran the length of her spine. His words echoed in her ears like a grim prophecy. She swallowed and said flatly, 'It would be my duty.'

'That's how I feel.' His broad shoulders lifted in a shrug. 'So it's no use complaining about it. In royal families duty is destiny, and it seems that my destiny is duty. Life takes odd turns.'

Beneath his dispassionate lack of self-pity Rosa sensed a flinty determination. Max wasn't a man to want or need sympathy; he'd face his future with the iron will and intelligence that had brought him success in his other endeavours.

Unable to find the right words to express her support and compassion, she said, 'How will you deal with your business commitments once you're King?'

Another pause, even longer this time, until he replied in a matter-of-fact voice. 'I won't—too much conflict of interest. I'm preparing to cash up and get out.' He looked across at her, his eyes level. 'That's confidential. I'll choose when to let the world know.'

'Of course,' she said automatically, while a small part of her warmed to the knowledge that he trusted her. How much would he miss the cut and thrust of big business, using the finely tuned entrepreneurial skills that had taken him to the top in such a short time?

Without thinking, she said, 'But there will always be the wine.'

And wished she'd kept quiet. Put like that, it sounded very second-best.

'I've already done as much for the industry as I can. They're ready to take charge of their own destiny. This outbreak of blight will sap their confidence, but once they've coped with it—and they will—they'll be fine.'

'I'm sure you've trained them well,' she said drily.

The corners of his beautiful mouth compressed into a brief smile. 'I always knew it wasn't going to be a lifetime commitment. Even before the succession problem came up I was getting ready to hand over. Of course I'll always have an interest in the industry—the fact that I own vine-yards in the valley will see to that.'

The car drew into the kerb and the bodyguard climbed out to open the back door. Passers-by—mostly tourists, Rosa realised as she got out—peered curiously at them.

Without any obvious hurry, Max took her arm. Sharp little thrills of electricity ran through her body, heating her skin; she had to stiffen her spine to meet the smiles and bows of the restaurant owner.

Control, she thought feverishly. You can control this! He was barely touching her, yet she felt it in every cell of her body—the innate, effortless authority of a man who combined steely brilliance as a businessman with the ability to match any of the grape-growers when it came to physical labour.

Their arrival was managed with the slickness of long experience, the owner seating them to one side of the room behind a screen of potted plants and a small fountain. They could see out, but few of the other diners even realised they were there, and fewer still knew who they were.

Rosa wondered what other women Max had brought to this place.

When they'd ordered he leaned back in his chair and smiled at her. Her skin tightened, and she tried to return his smile with one equally charming and enigmatic.

His face hardened and he looked down at the glass of wine he'd chosen for an aperitif, swirling it as he said idly, 'I'm glad you're enjoying New Zealand. What are your plans for the rest of your life?'

Bitter-sweet pleasure ached through her; she'd cherish the memory of this evening for the rest of her life. This would be the only time she'd ever sit like this with him, listen to him speak about something dear to his heart.

It would be all she had. When next she saw him he'd be officially recognised as the king's heir.

And as soon as the abdication process had taken place, he'd be the new King of Niroli.

Pain took her breath away. She loved him, she realised wretchedly. She'd always loved him. For some reason her heart had found another home when she was sixteen, and that suppressed love had grown despite the long, lonely years.

She managed a flippant smile. 'Find a way to

control shot blight first. After that—' she shrugged '—who knows? More of what I'm doing now— learning how to control anything that stops vine-growers producing their best results.'

Flushing, she met his probing green-gold gaze. An extraordinary sensation filled her, both buoyant and sad, exhilarating and poignant.

'Any ideas about your doctorate?'

'A few.' Tamping down her emotions, she told him some of the directions that interested her.

He listened intently, and made his own suggestions, impressing her with his knowledge of her world. They digressed to some of the projects she'd worked on; Rosa forcing herself to keep it light, her heart singing when he smiled at her tales of life in a laboratory.

'I can see you're happy,' he said as the first course arrived—pasta in a tangy tomato sauce, with the island's sharp cheese and scattered basil leaves making a fragrant topping. 'It's all you've ever wanted to do, isn't it?'

'And everything I've hoped for,' she said trying to sound both brisk and convincing, although the words echoed emptily through her mind. Setting her jaw, she changed the subject. 'This is a lovely place. Do you come here often?'

'Not as often as I used to,' he told her, before asking about her taste in books. From there they segued to the dangers of unfettered tourism the world over, the likelihood of the ice caps melting, the latest blockbuster film...

As course followed course—a crisp salad, then lamb roasted on a spit with rosemary and other island herbs, followed eventually by a magnificent fruit tart and coffee—Rosa let herself relax. Stimulated by his swift brain and trenchant opinions, she challenged him when she felt his views needed it, and in the process thoroughly enjoyed herself.

From beneath his lashes Max monitored the emotions playing across her face. This new Rosa—witty, sharp, sexy—fascinated him. Her quick brain and keen intelligence gave life to the subtle sensuousness of her features, and he relished her smile, and her laughter—soft and low and mischievous.

Although he'd always appreciated her sister Isabella's blonde loveliness, Rosa's dark bloom affected him on a more elemental level. Potent, intense, it bypassed the defences he'd erected against her, honing his awareness into a dangerously heady craving.

CHAPTER FOUR

THIS, Max decided, watching Rosa sip wine with delicate pleasure, had not been a good idea. He'd wanted to keep them both safe by spending the evening with other people around them; instead, he'd badly miscalculated. They were secluded behind the screen of greenery, a spell of intimacy woven around them, charging the air with crackling sexual awareness that tightened his gut and sent him to the border of craving.

Soon she'd leave Niroli; until she did, he had to keep this urgent appetite at bay. And as he'd never been one to let his libido control his will-power, why the hell was he so on edge?

Because this particular hunger—elemental, threatening to smash the constraints of will and logic—had never happened to him before.

And because the desire knotting his guts was

for his *cousin*. He intended to keep the promise he'd made to his—*their*—grandfather, which meant that Rosa was out of bounds: embargoed, prohibited, off limits and taboo.

But he'd make the most of this night, this rare communion of minds they'd discovered, because that would be all he'd ever have of her.

Alertly attuned to every inflection of his deep voice, every change in expression on his arrogant, lean face, Rosa sensed a subtle withdrawal.

'So where do you go from here?' she asked, forcing herself to sound only mildly interested. 'I assume Grandpapa will formally announce you as his heir soon.'

'Yes, very soon.'

'You'll be an excellent king—one entirely suited to the twenty-first century. Niroli is lucky to have you.'

One ironic black brow shot up. 'Thanks for the vote of confidence.'

It took more self-control than she knew she possessed, but she managed to produce a teasing, cousinly grin. 'You've coaxed, driven, convinced and charmed thousands of peasant grape-growers—who were perfectly happy with their outdated ways—into not only working together, but adopting modern methods. More, you were the brains behind the marketing campaign that brought their wine to the top of the world's best-seller lists. Ruling Niroli has to be a doddle compared to that.'

He leaned back in the chair, big and dominating and completely sure of himself, his smile almost mocking beneath the half-closed eyes that shielded his thoughts and emotions. 'I hope you're right. Are you ready to go?'

Chilled, she said, 'Yes,' in a colourless voice. Her lovely, enchanted evening was almost over. After this she'd live on dreams and memories.

Max looked up, and the waiter who'd spent the evening stationed discreetly some distance away so he could minister to their every need hurried towards them.

He bent deferentially and said something she couldn't quite catch. Max's brows met for a second, and in his face Rosa saw irritation, swiftly followed by a formidable, uncompromising assurance.

Frowning, he said to her, 'There's a crowd outside. Are you happy to go through it?'

After a second's hesitation, she nodded. 'It's been awhile. The last time…'

The last time she'd walked through a crowd had been at her parents' state funeral.

Max said curtly, 'We can go out the back way.'

Drawing in a sharp breath she said more strongly, 'No, it's all right. I'll be fine.'

He held her gaze with his, so keen and piercing she felt he could see into her soul. Then he said, 'I'll be with you.'

Oddly it almost sounded like a promise. Before Rosa had time to think about it, they'd reached the door and he took her arm. 'Smile,' he commanded, looking down at her. 'They don't mean you any harm.'

But he was alert—and, she sensed, angry at some deep, inner level. Obediently curving her lips, she went out with him onto the narrow pavement.

The crowd was made up mostly of the people of the city, gathering for a sight of their future king. Only a few tourists, made conspicuous by their clothes and curiosity, were scattered amongst them, watched with concealed interest by the two men she recognised as bodyguards.

People started clapping when they saw Max's tall figure. When they saw her there were even cries of, 'Ah, bella bella Rosita!'

Thank heavens she'd thought to pack a dinner dress! She waved back, her smile turning into a low gurgle of laughter when a young man flourished a bow in front of her and presented her with a rose, scarlet as sin, scented with a perfume that hung like the promise of seduction in the warm night air.

And then they were in the car, and Max leaned back, his profile arrogant and grim against the lights as the vehicle moved away.

'Sorry about that,' he said curtly, and reached over to take the rose from her and examine it.

'It's all right. I don't worry about the islanders.' She frowned. 'Surely you don't expect it to be booby-trapped?'

'Of course not,' he said, and handed it back.

But the little crowd, kindly though it was, had ruffled her. Born so long after the other royal children, more reserved and considerably less attractive than her older sister, she'd been raised out of the public eye. As soon as her parents had realised her fascination with science she'd followed Isabella to a Swiss boarding school where she'd just been another of the pupils—a princess, but also a nerd, tall and plain and awkward.

Well, she'd done something about that; she might not be anywhere near as beautiful as Isabella, or Max's lovers, but at least she didn't look like someone's poor relation anymore!

Without looking at her, Max said, 'You did well. What made me think you were shy? You show no signs of it now.'

'I don't think I am,' she said, surprised. 'It's just that Isabella was always the one who attracted attention. Fortunately she doesn't seem to mind it.'

'I remember you as a child—you used to look at the world with such solemn interest. It became a matter of pride for all of us when we were able to coax a smile from you. My mother used to say that still waters run deep, and that you were interesting.'

The words hung in the air, reminding her not only of the forbidden nature of any relationship, but the ten years between them.

She should thank him, because heat was

stealing like a swift, lethal poison through her veins. Surely something like this—this radiance—couldn't be wrong...

That was the excuse of the weak-willed, she told herself with stern ruthlessness as they got into the helicopter. Although loving Max mightn't be morally wrong, it was banned by the rules.

And it was useless. He'd made it more than clear that his duty was to Niroli.

She fought back her emotions, pretending to doze as the helicopter took them back to Cattina. Once inside the great hall of the castello she said sedately, 'Thank you for a wonderful evening, Max.'

'I should thank you.' But his smile didn't reach his eyes.

'Good night,' she said firmly, and walked towards the stairs. She had almost reached them when she heard him call her name.

Startled by the urgency in his voice, she turned, and saw him with a servant. 'What is it?' she asked, her heart speeding up to keep pace with her footsteps as she ran back. 'Grandpapa?'

'No. It looks as though another vineyard is afflicted.'

Her heart dropped. 'Hell!' she said fiercely.

His formidable features tightened. 'I know you're tired, but can you change and come with me?'

'Of course.'

Ten minutes later, clad in jeans and a shirt, she raced down the stairs. It had been warm in the capital, but here in the foothills it was crisp enough to warrant the jacket over her arm.

Max was on the telephone, speaking with clear precision. Rosa stopped just out of listening range, watching him, her eyes hungry beneath lowered lashes.

He was utterly gorgeous, she thought hungrily. Kate would swoon over him—and Max would probably respond to her with the sexual confidence of the experienced lover he was.

He looked up and beckoned her closer, his beautiful mouth compressing into a thin line as he demanded curtly, 'You're sure? Why wasn't I told?'

The answer clearly didn't please him. In a low, deadly voice he said, 'I'll speak to you tomorrow. Stay where you are.'

He snapped the telephone closed. Anger still

icing his words, he said, 'When the owner of the vineyard noticed the first shot holes he kept quiet and sprayed the vines with every spray he had. If one of the lab assistants hadn't come to take the tests you recommended yesterday we wouldn't have known about it until the vines started dying.'

She winced. 'Where is it? Close to the others?'

'No. On the other side of the valley.'

'Oh, God,' she whispered.

'Exactly. We'll meet Giovanni out at the vineyard.'

Neither spoke as he drove them there. Lights in windows in the small village a few hundred metres down the road indicated that the locals knew what had happened. Police were already guarding the gate and the disinfectant trough had been put in place; after a glance at Max's stony face they waved the vehicle through.

Inside the walled courtyard, Giovanni waited in a pool of light beside the owner and the rest of his household. As Rosa and Max got out of the car the white-haired patriarch squared his shoulders.

'I am sorry, Highness,' he said bleakly. 'Blame an old man's stubbornness.'

Max said, 'I don't blame. You stand to lose most by this.' Briefly he introduced him to Rosa.

'Your Highness,' the old man said with a bow that was close to courtly. 'It is always a delight to see you back on the island. Can you save my vines?'

'I doubt it,' she told him with sympathy, 'but we might be able to stop the disease spreading to cover the island.'

He spread his hands. 'It is a thing of the devil, this, but perhaps God sent you to help us.' He covered his grief with a sharp command to his wife to stop crying.

Max turned to the watchful group in the court-yard. 'Does anyone know of any other vines that might be affected?' he asked.

Through the general disclaimers, Max fixed one young man with a hard gaze. 'You have something to tell me?'

'Some of the vines at Papa Vitelli's do not look healthy,' the man said reluctantly. 'There are holes in the leaves…'

Max said, 'Thank you,' and spoke briskly into his phone.

That done, he surveyed the group of people,

keen gaze going from one concerned face to another. 'We need to know as soon as vines are found to be sick. We might be able to control this disease and save most of the vineyards, but if people hide the symptoms everyone will lose their vines. You have my word that, apart from the vineyards closest to the infected ones, no one will lose vines that are not sick, and that those who do will be helped to plant other crops until the ground is free from taint.'

There was a general shuffling of feet, but no one else volunteered information, and Rosa couldn't see signs of secret knowledge in any of the faces.

If she'd been a grape-grower she'd have told, she thought. Max had been frank, but an implacable note in his voice had ramped up her own tension. She wouldn't like to be the next grower who tried to conceal an outbreak.

If there was one...

Pray heaven there wasn't.

She picked up her kit and went to look at the vines; the technician had rigged up lights, and in their cold white glow she examined the leaves, her gut knotting as she recognised the signs.

'We don't need to wait for the test results. It's shot blight,' she said wearily.

Max turned to the grower. 'I am sorry, but they must be pulled out and burnt.'

The old man was silent, then he shrugged. 'So,' he said. 'I shall grow flowers until the ground is clean again.'

Rosa bent and kissed his cheek. 'There speaks a true islander,' she said quietly. 'Indomitable and brave as Hercules.'

'And blindly stubborn,' he countered ruefully, and everyone laughed a little.

On the way home Max said, 'That was well done, little cousin. He'll tell his great-grandchildren about that kiss.'

Irony tinged her smile. 'While they pick flowers. I feel so sorry for them. But at least they won't starve, as they might have fifty years ago.'

Dismissing her words with a shrug of his broad shoulders, Max asked, 'What about the Vitelli vines?'

'I can't be certain without lab tests, of course, but it certainly looks like the first stage of shot blight.' She concealed a massive yawn. 'I wish I could find out what vector spreads it.'

'You and me both,' he said grimly, pulling up in the castello forecourt.

A chill little wind echoed Rosa's emotions as she got out. She huddled further into her coat, and Max said instantly, 'You're cold.'

'Not really.'

Brows drawn together, he examined her face. She looked pinched, her lush mouth held under such firm control that he had to stifle a wild impulse to kiss it into relaxation.

'And you're exhausted,' he said decisively. 'Come into the study and I'll pour you a drink. You need to wind down before you get to bed—otherwise you'll stay awake all night with your mind racing around in circles.'

When she couldn't hide her surprise he felt a pang of remorse. His blatant physical response to the grown-up Rosa had shocked him into withdrawal, and he must have seemed cold and aloof. Poor kid—except that she was no longer a kid in spite of her untouched air.

Could she possibly still be a virgin? Shocked by the primitive response that question aroused, he wished he could take back his suggestion. Thoughts of initiating her into the manifold pleasures of love-making were a distraction he couldn't afford.

'Thank you,' she said, her husky tone sliding through his defences, seductive as honey and wine. 'I'd like that. No coffee, though.'

Max led the way into a comfortable study where a fire flared golden light on the tall book-shelves around the wall. With easy, graceful strides, Rosa went across to the fire and held out her long fingers to it.

Max banished a tantalising image of those elegant hands on his skin. 'No coffee,' he agreed in a clipped voice. 'You're already wired.'

He poured brandy into two glasses and handed one to her, cursing inwardly when their fingers came in contact. Next time use a tray, he told himself as his whole body tightened in a clamour of primitive hunger.

Better still, make sure there is no next time.

'Thank you,' she said in a subdued voice, her lashes hiding her thoughts.

She looked around and put the glass down on the small table by the chair. 'It's lovely and warm in here,' she said, and peeled off her jacket.

Max had to stop himself from helping her, but

he could no longer trust his reactions to her closeness. A hooded glance at her maddeningly serene face revealed that she was quite unaware of the way her clothes clung provocatively to her breasts and her narrow waist, and the long, pleasingly racy line of her thighs and legs.

Turning abruptly away, he stopped himself from gulping his brandy and noted with ironic detachment that his hand shook when he set the glass down with a surprisingly sharp chink. Alcohol was probably the worst thing he could drink right now. His body was on fire with the elemental desire to kiss her sensuous mouth until it softened in reciprocated desire.

He understood basic sexual attraction—hell, he'd succumbed to it a couple of times in his youth, letting his hormones run away with his common sense. He'd despised himself, and since then he'd been more discriminating, seeking a meeting of minds beyond the heated excitement of sex.

But this was something else again. Ever since Rosa had come to the castello he'd been walking a knife-edge, feeling his self-discipline crumble under the onslaught of her innocence and charm.

A taut awareness sharpened the silence. Did she sense it? Max watched her take a small, delicate sip of the liquid. He wanted her more than he'd wanted any other woman.

And although she didn't realise it, she was giving off signals.

'This is delicious,' she said in a smoky voice. 'Is it made on the island?'

'I'm glad you like it. The distillery is our latest project.' He sounded abrupt, so he wasn't surprised when she turned away from him. 'Sit down.'

After a cool, challenging glance from beneath lifted brows, she obeyed. 'You sound like the principal of my school when she wanted to tell me something bad,' she said primly, but an uneven edge to her voice gave her away.

Recklessly pleased by her unspoken aware-ness, Max reined in the rampaging urges of his body and sat down opposite her, keeping his gaze fixed on her face.

That didn't work either. Sleepiness and the brandy had given her eyes a heavy-lidded look, unconsciously seductive, and her mouth was full and pink and more than luscious.

If she'd been using tricks he might have withstood her appeal better, but she clearly didn't understand what she was doing to him. He felt like an old, decadent roué, whipping up his jaded appetite with youth and freshness.

Only there was nothing jaded about this. Silently cursing his unruly body, he clamped down on its demands and forced his mind back to the reason she was there. 'So what is your advice?'

She hesitated, thinking of the two elderly men who had faced a bleak future without their vines. 'You know what it is. Tear out the vines and burn them. Do the same to the adjoining vineyards. Fumigate the ground and use the antibiotic I brought on all the others around. Monitor every vine in the valley every week, and repeat the whole process whenever a new infection is found.'

Mouth compressed into a hard line, he swirled brandy around in his glass, watching the amber liquid shimmer and gleam in the light of the fire. She kept her lashes lowered, but through them she could see his hard, handsome face, compelling, resolute, stamped with unwavering authority.

He looked up at that, and she met his gaze, more gold than green. Grimly determined, he said, 'How long will the supplies of antibiotic last?'

Frowning, she admitted, 'Two more outbreaks.'

'How long do you suggest we monitor the rest of the vineyards?'

'For at least a year,' she said steadily. 'If you like, I'll make out a programme of each step that has to be taken.'

'Thank you. How high-tech will this monitoring be?'

'Anyone with high-school science could do it, provided they're conscientious. I've spoken to the head of the lab here; his number-crunchers will check the results. Would it be possible to get high-school seniors to do it?'

His brows lifted. 'You can say *"high school seniors"* and *"conscientious"* in almost the same breath?' he asked, deadpan.

That surprised a gurgle of laughter from her, but she soon sobered. 'I'm sure you can find enough sensible kids to make it work. They'd have to be supervised, of course.'

'Giovanni can organise that. He knows everyone here very well indeed.'

Together they worked out a plan of campaign, more urgently needed now in the light of this last outbreak. The next day Max would supervise the destruction of the infected vineyards, while Rosa would check out those that had won a reprieve.

When she gave another prodigious yawn, Max got to his feet. 'Time for bed. I can only hope that before long you come up with something that kills the blight without the destruction of so many vines.'

She said with a touch of acid, 'Believe me, we're trying.'

'Not fast enough.'

The self-mockery in his tone made her smile sardonically. 'I know, but it's not a fast process. People hear about miracle breakthroughs, but what they don't realise is that they're often based on twenty—sometimes fifty—years of research and experiment.'

'I know,' he said abruptly, and drained his brandy glass. He glanced at her shocked face, and smiled without humour. 'It's all right; I'm not going to drink myself into a stupor—I've never been an advocate of quick fixes.'

'I wouldn't blame you,' she said, setting down her own barely touched glass. She didn't need alcohol's spurious warmth; she was hot enough already. 'I don't imagine you're looking forward to telling those grape-growers that you're burning their livelihood and the vines their great-grandfathers worked.'

He shrugged and got up, stretching. Acutely conscious of the power contained within his tall, lithe body, she clambered to her feet, her nerves jumping in an overload of sensation.

Perhaps it was the brandy, perhaps the fire, perhaps a return to adolescent clumsiness, but one of her legs gave way slightly so she had to grab the back of the chair to balance herself.

Max covered the distance between them in a long stride and gripped her shoulders. 'Are you all right?'

'Of course I am,' she said, but her voice had an odd dreamy inflection.

Realising the danger too late, she shook her head abruptly, stiffening when she tried to pull away from the dangerous challenge of Max's embrace.

He reacted as though she'd thrown down some gauntlet. His arms tightened around her, bringing her in sharp, violently subversive contact with his lean, aroused body. Breath catching in her throat, she looked up into a face suddenly hard-hewn and demanding, eyes glittering green-gold gems against olive skin, a slash of dark colour along the conqueror's cheekbones.

He said something beneath his breath, and her eyes widened in shock as he bent his head and kissed her.

The kiss lasted only for a second. But even though Max lifted his head as though he'd taken poison from her lips, he didn't let Rosa go.

Dazed and boneless, she had to fight the almost overwhelming impulse to lean her head on his broad shoulder and offer solace in the only way she knew—with the warmth and softness of her body.

Except that she didn't know how. She'd been kissed, but she'd never given herself to a man. Besides, she thought bleakly, Max wasn't a man to take comfort in casual encounters.

Or forbidden ones.

'That wasn't sensible,' she said, her voice stark and shocked.

She tried to pull herself upright, to look him in the face and demand that he let her go, but the words wouldn't come and she couldn't summon the will to move.

His hands slid from her shoulders to her back, holding her a hair's breadth away from the strength and warmth she craved with a desperation that fogged her brain.

'Rosa,' he said thickly, gold lights overwhelming the green of his eyes. 'Bella Rosita…'

CHAPTER FIVE

PRETTY *little Rose...*

It was heaven. Shivering with tantalising anticipation, Rosa turned her face into the column of Max's throat, delicately inhaling a combination of wood-smoke and the rich aroma of brandy, and a faint, enticingly potent scent that had to be personal to his body.

She sighed.

In a voice she'd never heard from him before—a raw, reckless voice—he said, 'I should never have said that.' When she didn't move, he added roughly, 'Rosa, we have to stop.'

And the perilous haze of sensual desire lifted enough for her to realise that not only was he very aroused, but that he was furious.

As he had every right to be. Shame flooded her, stripping away every emotion except desperate pride. For both of them it would be best if she pretended to take this lightly.

She dragged in a jagged breath. 'Then let me go.' But it was a plea, not a command.

Every muscle in his big body contracted in fierce resistance. Rosa held her breath. Heady desire weakened her; if he didn't let her go she'd surrender.

And just when it seemed inevitable, his formidable will won out over the elemental instinct to possess, and he released her.

It took all of her courage to step back, look him in the eyes and say with a tight smile, 'I'm sorry, I must be more tired than I thought.'

His answering smile was cynical. It hurt her in some hidden part of her heart, but she met it with squared shoulders and her head held high.

'Both of us,' he said, tacitly accepting her refusal to allow the kiss any importance. 'Sleep in as long as you like tomorrow morning.'

But she spent the night twisting and tossing, her willful mind going over and over the incandescent moments when his lips had possessed hers and she'd been transported into a world where nothing mattered but Max…

When at last she woke silence pressed down on her. She lay listening to it as slow, painful tears gathered behind her eyelids.

She'd betrayed herself as openly and obviously as if she'd told him that she loved him and wanted him.

After those precious few moments in his arms, the tenuous friendship she'd thought they'd forged had vanished beneath Max's mask of chilly formality. From now on he'd call her *little cousin* all the time, and remind her at least once a day of the family rule that said no blood relatives could marry.

Yet he'd wanted her. Even as something wild and unregenerate in her thrilled at that thought, she banished it. It would be stupid to fool herself into believing his desire was anything more than the casual lust any man would feel when a warm, compliant body was pressed against him.

But she'd always remember his harsh indrawn breath, the subtle hardening of his body against hers, the sudden increase in his heart rate...

And her flowering of excited confidence when she'd realised she could feel passion.

But only for this man, she thought bleakly.

Abruptly her tears overflowed. Although she knew no one could hear her through the solid stone walls of her room, she buried her head under the pillow until her eyes dried. Eventually she fell into a restless sleep punctuated by snatches of desperate erotic dreams where Max came to her and everything miraculously was all right...

Except that each time he turned on her in nightmare contempt, and she woke to the sound of her shattered breathing.

When she came down in the morning Giovanni was waiting for her, his face worried.

She smiled and tried to sound light-hearted. 'I'm sorry I'm late. I slept in.'

But she knew his keen eyes had noticed the ravages of the night through the cosmetics she'd applied.

He gave a stiff little bow. 'The prince is helping the growers destroy their vines. He suggested that after you eat I take you around so that you can explain both to me and to the owners what needs to be done for the vineyards in the infected areas.'

Rosa fought back a sinful pleasure that Max had thought of her. 'It's not difficult, but every vine needs to be checked and tested every week. Max seems doubtful that there are enough suitable people here to do that, but I'll make a checklist so that all they need to do is tick or cross a box. Anyone who is used to working with vines can do that.'

'Everybody in Cattina has grown up with vines,' Giovanni told her with a tired smile. 'They are like our sisters and our brothers. The prince said you suggested high school students, but there are plenty of people around who will do this, especially as the prince says they will be paid. People here know what this blight can do, so it is up to us to find a way to kill it.'

It was a long day and an emotional one. The vine-growers hid their fears beneath a gruff friendliness, but smoke from the huge bonfires drifted over the valley in thick clouds, a threat to everything these people had worked so hard to achieve. Ignoring it, Rosa gritted her teeth and went grimly on examining each vine.

At lunch Giovanni took her to his house and introduced her to a pretty girl busy in the kitchen. 'Elena has cooked us lunch,' he said with pride that surprised Rosa.

Most of the island girls learned to cook at their mother's knees, helping in the kitchen almost before they went to school. 'I'm looking forward to it,' Rosa said with a smile.

Elena, a slim, willowy woman with a calm, serene face, smiled too. 'Perhaps Giovanni should tell you that I'm blind,' she said without a hint of self-pity in her tone.

Rosa squelched an involuntary spasm of compassion, instinct warning her it would be rejected. This woman, with her sleek, chic hair and her air of cool, patient competence, didn't need anything like pity.

She said cheerfully, 'So?'

It was the right answer. Elena's laughter was genuine and unforced, although Giovanni looked taken aback.

'Thank you, Highness,' Elena said.

Elena joined them for the meal, talking little until Rosa set herself the task of drawing the other woman out, learning that she was an excellent pianist who'd chosen to use her talents as a music therapist.

The food was superb. When the meal was finished, Rosa thanked her and said, 'If I ever come back to live on Niroli, perhaps you can teach me to cook.'

Elena grinned. 'There are others who could do that much better than I, but if you'd like to learn the piano…?'

Rosa gave a theatrical sigh. 'My mother used to weep when I played, wondering how on earth she'd ever had such a fumble-fingered child. I love listening to it, but I'll leave its execution to those with talent.'

Breaking in, Giovanni said, 'Highness, why don't you rest until the sun loses a little of its heat? You were up most of last night, and you've been on your feet all morning—you must be tired.'

The idea appealed enormously. Weariness weighed her down and she'd lost her ability to cope with Niroli's summer sun, the lion sun as the islanders called it. But she shook her head.

'I have to get this over and done with. It's too painful for the growers—they need to be told as soon as possible, not spend days waiting for the axe to fall.'

He said, 'You are not used to this.'

'If Prince Max can do it, I can. It's much worse for him, and worst of all for the growers.'

'That is why he is with them, working like a slave to get the vines out of the ground.'

She smiled at the note of pride in Giovanni's voice. There was no doubt about the affection between these two men.

'He's a good man,' she said quietly.

Elena nodded. 'A very good man. And if you will excuse me, Highness, I will go now.'

Rosa smiled and they said their goodbyes, Elena disappearing into the cool interior and she and Giovanni walked out onto the terrace outside.

He looked across at the horizon, where a fresh plume of thick, dark smoke announced yet another fire. 'Only Prince Max could have persuaded these men to tear their vines from the ground and burn them. They trust him because he has kept every promise he made to them.'

Carefully modulating her tone, Rosa said, 'He'll be a good king.'

Giovanni looked sharply at her, his eyes shadowed by the brim of his hat. 'Yes,' he said after a moment, 'he will make an excellent king. The islanders are happy that he is the next one.'

* * *

Dusk was falling when she got back to the castle. In the late afternoon a breeze had sprung up to carry most of the smoke away, but the last of the fires was still blazing against the hills, its flames greedily consuming the vines. Max was nowhere in sight, and the manservant told her he hadn't come home.

Rosa showered the smoke from her body and her hair, pulled on her dressing gown, and emerged to discover the maid scooping up her smutty, smelly clothes. The woman's eyes were red.

'What's wrong?' Rosa asked, heart clamping.

'My father had to burn all his vines today, even though they were not infected with this disease.'

'I'm so sorry,' Rosa said quietly, wishing vainly there were something she could do to ease this pain.

'Why?' the maid asked, driven by pain to ignore convention and quiz a member of the royal family. 'These vines are our ancestors'— why were they slaughtered like this when there was nothing wrong with them?'

Rosa explained, and gradually the maid grew calmer. 'I understand,' she said wearily, wiping eyes that had filled again. 'But—it is cruel.'

Rosa nodded, her own face bleak. 'Yes,' she said. 'Sometimes life is cruel.'

The maid looked at her. 'For you too?' she said in a disbelieving tone.

'For everyone,' Rosa said. 'You have your father and mother.'

The older woman flushed. 'Idiot that I am, I had forgotten,' she said, and stepped forward, enfolding Rosa in a hug. 'Poor little one—to lose them so swiftly, so early.'

Then, embarrassed, she dropped her arms, gathered up the clothes again and almost ran from the room.

Gratefully Rosa got into a fresh outfit, a slim-fitting pair of trousers and a sleek top in garnet-red, and went down the stairs.

The manservant came to meet her when she reached the great hall. 'The prince asked me to tell you that he won't be back for dinner,' he said. 'I have set the table for you in the small dining room unless you would prefer to eat in your room?'

'The small dining room would be lovely, thank you.' She didn't want to be shut in her room.

Although dinner was delicious, Rosa ate mechanically and without appetite. Afterwards she wandered into the study where Max had given her brandy, and took down a book from the shelves, hoping to drive out of her rogue mind the brief, fiery moments when he'd held her and kissed her.

The book was a children's classic, one she'd loved and lost somewhere along the way. She sank down into a chair and began to read.

Max walked down the stone staircase. He'd showered away the reek of sweat and smoke from his body, but he suspected that the smell of the ancient vines burning would be in his nostrils for ever, like the weight on his soul of the growers' grief and pain and fear.

Yet they had trusted him. And Rosa...

He pushed the door into the study open and stopped, hit by such relief and pleasure that the memories of the day vanished.

She was asleep, her head curved against the arm of a winged chair. And she was smiling. No cosmetics hid her silken skin, and although her hair had been tied into a loose knot, it had pulled free to tumble in an inviting black flood over one slender shoulder. The rich garnet-crimson shirt revealed the elegant lines of her body, and her long legs were stretched out in front of her, slim ankles relaxed.

Max almost turned away, but he fought down the exhilarating tide of adrenaline and set his jaw. Now that he knew how sweet she felt in his arms, all he wanted to do was gather her up and hold her, lose himself in her warmth and her sweetness and give in to the reckless need that gripped him.

Last night should never have happened, but she'd treated his kiss the best way—as an unimportant aberration.

So he'd wake her gently, be as indifferent and remote as he could be, and he'd make sure that they didn't touch—not even fingertips—ever again.

Poker in hand, he reached into the fireplace and stirred the embers, making as much noise as he could. Then he piled more wood onto the fire, dusting his hands as he stood up.

She was awake, her sleepy gaze lingering on him with vulnerable intensity.

'Max,' she said drowsily, as though he was everything she needed in her life.

And she smiled, a lazy smile that held an undercurrent of hunger.

Sheer, potent passion gripped him with talons both painful and compelling. Every muscle tightened at an image of waking to the sight of her, sleek and sated, in his bed, with that exact soft, addictive smile.

He concealed his body's betrayal by sitting down in an armchair opposite her and asking in his most matter-of-fact tone, 'How did your day go?'

'As well as could be expected,' she said, her voice slow and husky. 'Better than yours, I imagine; at least I was dealing with people who hoped their vines would be safe.'

Max recalled an old woman who'd shrieked her agony as the bulldozers bit into the stony ground. She'd turned to him and said bitterly, 'Anyone else I would curse, but you—you would not put us through this if you didn't know it had to be done.'

'I'm always surprised at their trust,' he said. 'It's taken time, and it would never have happened without Giovanni to vouch for me from the beginning.'

'They'd have come to trust you eventually.'

Don't, he wanted to snarl. Don't look at me

like that, with glowing appreciation as though I'm some sort of god. It tempts me beyond bearing.'

He said with cool detachment, 'I doubt it. He stood sponsor until they accepted me, but this—' He stopped abruptly, letting his hands indicate his emotions. 'This is so much to ask of them.'

'It has to be done.' Because he was gazing at the flames, Rosa let herself examine his face, hardened by weariness. 'In their hearts they know that.'

'Having you here made a big difference.'

Astonished, Rosa asked, 'Why? They don't know *me*. Except for holidays, I've been away at school and then at university since I was a child.'

'You came to help them,' he said, his eyes still fixed on the fire. 'They won't forget that. Neither will I.'

She turned her head away so he couldn't see the soft colour that heated her cheeks. She didn't want to be remembered for doing her duty, damn it!

In a tone that came close to curtness, he said, 'And now, if you'll excuse me, I'm going up to bed. You look tired too, so I'd suggest an early night.'

Chilled, she scrambled to her feet. The barriers against her were locked in place again; their fragile relationship was out of bounds.

And although she tried to tell herself that it was for the best, she had to struggle with a flash of mutiny before she could say, 'Have you had dinner?'

'I ate with Giovanni at his place.'

Had Elena cooked it for him? Rosa repressed the shoddy spark of jealousy as he went on, 'I hope you had a pleasant, if solitary, meal.'

He spoke with the cool politeness of a host, and for both of their sakes she had to accept it and return it. 'It was lovely, thank you.'

That got her to the door. But her heart was splintering slowly, crumbling into small shards of pain.

'Do you want to take the book with you?' he asked, picking it up from the chair, where it must have fallen while she'd slept.

'Oh—thank you.'

He handed it over, and before his black lashes shut out his thoughts she saw a glint of golden fire in the depths of his eyes. Ignoring the swift, futile lift of her heart, she headed for the door, clutching the book as though it held the secrets of the universe.

Side by side, but not touching, they walked up the stairs, filling the silence with discussion about future tactics for fighting the outbreak.

At her door he said, 'Good night.'

Rosa gave a bleak little smile, keeping her gaze on his chin. She didn't dare meet his eyes, and she certainly wasn't going to look at his mouth.

He said harshly, 'Stop looking so tragic. It isn't the end of the world.'

'It might be for the grape-growers.'

'They're the descendants of survivors; they'll keep going because they've got guts and determination and a sense of what's due to *their* descendants.'

This wasn't about the islanders.

Rosa understood what he was telling her, and her whole being rose in rebellion. 'If they have any,' she said, a catch in her voice.

Tension—taut as steel wire—stretched between them.

'They will,' he said grimly. And when she didn't answer he stated, 'Any other way is cowardly, Rosa.'

Not daring to speak because her voice would reveal too much of her turbulent emotions, she shook her head and turned to go into her room.

'Rosa!' He caught her arm, swivelling her around to face him.

She looked up, eyes bright with unshed tears. Max's angular, aristocratic features clamped into an arrogant mask, and then he swore, low and ferocious through gritted teeth, and pulled her into his arms, crushing her against him with the full force of his strength.

Stunned, she lifted a hand and touched his cheek, her fingers lingering as glittering sparks of anticipation raced through her bloodstream.

'It's all right,' she whispered, not really knowing what she was saying. 'Max, I'll be fine.'

'I know,' he muttered, his voice deep and driven, and kissed her with an unrestrained passion that should have scared the wits out of her.

But this was Max, and she loved him. Her mouth softened beneath his demand, then staked its own claim, every bit as hungry and compelling as his.

Shuddering at the impact of his unique scent in

her nostrils, his taste in her mouth, his body urgent with a reckless appetite, Rosa surrendered to the prompting of her own blazing need.

Mindlessly she met the sensual thrust of his hips when he gathered her even closer to kiss the corners of her lips. She groaned with helpless excitement as he traced the length of her throat with his seeking mouth; she had never felt so vulnerable, or so safe.

She let herself lace her hands in his hair, delighting in the silken warmth against her skin. Desire drummed between them, an insistent drive beneath the wildfire anticipation of being close to him.

And when he stroked her breast, then cupped its soft weight, turbulent arousal rioted through her, swift and fierce as a forest fire, burning away every last tiny shred of inhibition…

Max froze. The seething carnality ebbed, and an unbearable silence fell around them. Rosa's breath blocked her lungs. Moving slowly, carefully, he put her away from him and stepped back, the hands that fell to his sides clenching into fists.

Rosa looked up into a face as stony as the

bronze warrior he so resembled. Her heart dropped in endless free fall.

He said tonelessly, 'I am sorry for that. I seem to be saying this far too often, but it should never have happened.'

She should accept the apology, pretend that those kisses, that searing tide of emotion, meant nothing. Then life would go on as it had for years. They would avoid each other at official functions, make sure they never met at any other time.

She said tersely, 'I know, but it did. What are we going to do about it?'

His hooded gaze, hard as quartz, didn't flicker. 'Nothing,' he said. 'Not now, not ever.'

And he turned and left her standing alone, as she would always be from now on, watching him walk away.

Gulping, she opened her door and fled into the safety of her room.

But once there, frustrated adrenalin surging set her to pacing the floor. And because anything was easier to bear than grief, she let anger take its place, fuming because life was so utterly unfair.

Why should she be so stupid as to want the one man she couldn't have?

She stopped in front of the mirror and stared at the woman reflected there—a stranger with bright, sleepy eyes, her mouth eager and red and tender from Max's kisses...

That primal stimulation still thrummed through her body, making her dizzy with reckless longing. Her skin felt too tight, her clothes dragging at it with erotic effect, stirring up sensations she'd never experienced before. Beneath the material of her shirt her nipples were tightly budded, prepared for an ecstasy she'd never know.

She closed her eyes and turned away.

Max wanted her—although not enough to let his desire overwhelm his integrity.

It was knowledge for which she'd paid a bitter price, because it made his rejection so much harder to bear. If only they weren't cousins, if only he weren't the next King of Niroli...

'If only you could find a way to save the world from war and violence,' she muttered savagely at her reflection. 'Even if only you could find a cure for shot blight. It's not going to happen, so forget it.'

Tears sprang into her eyes. Dashing them away, she resumed pacing. It would take at least two weeks to see whether the precautionary measures were working.

She had to prove she was as strong as Max, who'd rejected her so comprehensively—for all the right reasons, she reminded herself bitterly. And once she'd left Niroli, she wouldn't see him again until his coronation, and after that it would be at his wedding to some ideal candidate with the right bloodlines.

Who would that be? With his ruthless good looks and sophistication and his magnetism, Max could choose any woman in the world for his bride.

But it would probably be the elegant Scandinavian princess with whom his name had been linked.

Or the beautiful American heiress…

Rosa stripped off her clothes, pulled on her nightclothes and crawled into bed. Hideous pictures of each exquisite blonde paraded mockingly behind her eyes. She pulled the covers around her and resolutely recited the periodic table until the clamour in her body settled to a manageable level and she finally slept.

After another wretched night she woke to a cloudy sky and the prospect of rain—rain that might spread the infestation. At least it gave her something else to worry about, she told herself forlornly, then mentally chided herself for being so selfish. All she had was a cracked heart; the islanders were facing the destruction of a way of life that had lasted for over two thousand years.

Whatever, she had people to train and a report to write for the lab back in New Zealand.

The next few days flew by. Apart from at dinner, when Max made sure they were chaperoned by guests, she saw little of him. Giovanni escorted her around the vineyards, and she found herself growing quite fond of the elderly man. It even hurt a little that he seemed to have some reservations about her.

She didn't see Elena again, and when she asked Giovanni he told her that she had gone back home.

On a warm, clear day towards the end of the week Max flew to Porto Di Castellante to talk to his grandfather. Rosa would have liked to go too, but she wasn't surprised when he told her that the king had strength for only one visit a day.

'He must be very frail,' she said anxiously before Max left, trying not to watch as he picked up a slim leather briefcase from a table at the foot of the stairs.

This was Max in another persona—the cool, astute businessman who'd not only parlayed the fortune he'd inherited into a position of power and untold wealth, but also master-minded the campaign that saw the wines of Niroli reach the top.

'Physically,' Max agreed. He inspected his mobile phone and tucked it into his pocket. Then he gave her a sharp glance. 'He's not deliberately keeping you dangling. He fully intends to see you before you go.'

'I know,' she said, adding with a wry twist to her lips, 'Just as I know that for Grandpapa women shouldn't aspire to be more than deco-rations when they're young, and then the mothers of sons.'

Max nodded. 'I'm afraid he's irretrievably stuck in the nineteenth century, but it's not personal. He loves you.'

Touched, she smiled a little mistily at him. 'I know,' she said. 'Do you know what he gave me for Christmas? The most magnificent diamond necklace, and a set of antique scales, exquisitely balanced.'

Since the night they'd kissed Max had treated her with either avuncular friendliness or aloof detachment, so his swift grin warmed her heart.

He said drily, 'Let me guess—the necklace is in a vault somewhere, while you use the scales at work?'

'You know me too well,' she admitted, laughing.

Time froze; they looked at each other, and for an instant she saw a kind of bitter longing in his eyes. Voice trembling, she said, 'It's all right. I'll be gone soon.'

'You're never gone,' he said as though the words were torn from him. 'But it's impossible—unthinkable.'

Her heart gave a sudden leap. For a second she allowed herself to really feel what his words meant. 'Unthinkable,' she repeated numbly.

'You're so young—one day you'll meet a man who'll raise your temperature and make you laugh, a man you'll like as well as want. A man who'll be what I can never be—your husband.'

She shook her head.

'Yes,' he said, his flat, lethal tone telling her more than his words. 'It must happen.'

'And you?'

He shrugged, his face closing against her. 'As always,' he said evenly, 'I'll do my duty.'

'Max—'

'No.' He turned away from her and walked across the great hall towards the huge front doors.

CHAPTER SIX

GIOVANNI made his way into the great hall from the kitchen, where he'd been drinking coffee with the cook. Now on his way to join the prince, he blinked when he saw Princess Rosa, her white, strained face shuttered against a grief so intense she hadn't even noticed him as she'd hurried up the stairs.

Frowning, he stopped in the shadow of one of the great pillars and switched his attention to Prince Max, standing just inside the doors.

The prince was looking after her, his normal relentless control over his expression loosened. In that proud, masterful face Giovanni saw the bleak confirmation of his suspicion. The older man lowered his gaze, something tightening painfully in his chest.

Almost immediately the prince said curtly, 'Ah, Giovanni. Are you ready?'

Giovanni met his cool, commanding scrutiny. 'The helicopter is ready, and so am I,' Giovanni said quietly. He had to think—but not now, not here.

Back in her room, Rosa forced herself to face reality. It seemed that she was a one-woman man; if she couldn't have Max then she didn't want any other. And as it was impossible—*unthinkable!*—to have Max, she'd never marry, never bear the children she'd always seen in her future.

At least she had her work.

But even that let her down. Science had been her passion, yet for the first time the day dragged—because Max wasn't there.

Late in the afternoon she spent an hour talking to the people who were going to check the vines; young and enthusiastic, they crowded around her, asking questions and absorbing her comments. Giovanni had been right; she hadn't needed to impress on them the importance of regular, accurate record-keeping. They were the sons and daughters of grape-growers; they knew what was at stake.

Siesta time had been taken up with intensive discussions with the lab technicians, suggesting things that could be implemented to further safeguard the vines, revealing the current thinking on shot blight and its possible causes.

It was almost dark when she walked back to the castello, and she realised that unconsciously she'd been waiting all day for the sound of the helicopter. How dreary was that! She pushed up the collar of her coat and shivered. Max had probably decided to stay in Porto di Castellante.

It was better that he should. His admission that morning still ached in her heart. Oh, his iron-bound sense of duty meant that he hadn't revealed his feelings in words, and she didn't fool herself that he loved her. But she'd always treasure that stark statement.

You're never gone.

How many women had had a declaration of desire and a rejection delivered at the same time?

Probably millions, she thought wearily. If only she could fight for her love—but she couldn't re-arrange their fates to suit herself. The stark truth was that Max was her cousin and also the future King of Niroli, the last male heir. Niroli needed him, and what was her one little life in the scheme of things compared to the welfare of the millions of people who looked to him for their future?

Hands deep in her pockets, she lifted her head sharply, sure she heard the distinctive *chop-chop-chop* of the helicopter's rotors.

Excitement rode her hard, bringing colour to her cheeks and a fleeting, excited smile. She started across the road to the castello, hearing—too late—the agitated tooting of a car horn. After a moment's flaring pain as she was hit and hurled into the air, darkness swallowed her up.

Max looked at the lights of the little city below, thinking over his interview with the king. Their relationship had always been rocky; as a kid he'd thought it personal, but growing up had changed his mind. The king's favourite grandchildren were those from his first—and dearly loved—wife. He wasn't nearly so attached to those from his second wife.

Max understood why. Basically cold, his grandmother was driven by ambition, a trait she'd passed onto her only child. Max's father had never reconciled himself to being born second in line to the throne, and then demoted even further by his half-brother's sons.

Shrugging, Max eased the tension in his shoulders. He and his grandfather had discussed constitutional matters, and then the old man had startled him by raising the subject of a wife.

'Do you have any preferences?' he'd asked.

'No,' Max said shortly.

His grandfather snorted. 'Well, you'd better start looking. You've been living like a monk this past year or so. It's not normal.'

Max lifted his brows. 'I've been busy,' he said, more mildly than he felt. The old man looked grey and drawn, as though he was holding himself together by stern will-power. 'And now there's this disease in the vines.'

'How's young Rosa doing?'

'Extremely well, but she's giving no guarantees of success.' Briefly he outlined the steps he'd taken and Rosa's suggestions for confining the outbreak.

The king nodded. 'Doctors or not, I'll see her when she comes here on her way back to New Zealand,' he said. 'I'm feeling better by the day.'

And that had been an end to it, but just before

Max had left the king had said in a different voice from his usual autocratic tones, 'Give the prospect of marriage some thought. Niroli needs heirs—plenty of them, and the sooner the better.'

He was right. Max watched the lights of Cattina come up to greet them as the helicopter descended. The decision of his various grandsons to choose their own paths of life had appalled the king. Max was certainly not the man he'd have chosen to follow him on the throne, but the old autocrat had grudgingly accepted that there was no one else.

If he turned it down, the only person left was Rosa.

And even if the people of Niroli could be persuaded to accept a woman as their monarch, the family rules applied equally to her.

Duty or love—the age-old dilemma. Realising that his hand was clenched into a fist on the arm of the seat, he relaxed his fingers.

She was young enough to get over this...this wilderness of passion and aching, tormenting need. His mobile mouth pulled into a grim smile. Who was he fooling? He'd had five years to deal with it, and it hadn't gone for him.

But she was resilient and strong. Eventually another man would convert that innocent sensuousness into rapturous satisfaction.

Max discovered he was grinding his teeth. Bleakly he told himself he'd be glad when at last she was happily married.

And knew he lied.

The chopper touched down gently, the clatter of the rotors changing pitch. Max frowned. There seemed to be a welcoming committee—surely, he thought with a stab of fear, not another outbreak? He searched the knot of people for Rosa's tall elegant figure, but couldn't find it. His concern eased. If it had been another case of shot blight she'd be waiting.

He picked up his briefcase and got out, bending his head until he was well beyond the clattering rotors.

The mayor bobbed his awkward bow. 'Your Highness,' he shouted, 'it is the princess—she has been hit by a car.'

In a voice no one had ever heard before, Max demanded, 'What are her injuries?'

The mayor said hastily, 'Slight.' He crossed himself. 'Bruises only, not even a broken arm or leg, but she has concussion and the doctor says she needs a nurse for a couple of days. One is with her now, and the doctor also.'

'Thank you,' Max said, long legs taking him towards the castello. Behind him he could hear the mayor telling Giovanni how it happened; one part of his mind heard it, but the other was concentrated on his cousin, in pain and suffering.

Rosa lay quietly, mainly because her head hurt too much to formulate thoughts. She knew she'd been run into, knew she'd only been bruised and that this headache was a mild case of concussion.

If this was mild, she'd hate to have a serious one.

And it didn't help to know that she'd been to blame; hearing the chopper had temporarily turned off her brain.

Soft noises lifted her eyelids; she stared at Max's beloved face, and sudden tears clogged her lashes. 'Don't make me cry,' she whispered. 'My head is killing me.'

A warm, strong hand clasped hers. He said uncompromisingly, 'When you've recovered *I'll* kill you. What possessed you to walk across the street without looking? No, don't answer that—you're in pain.'

'It's just a headache,' she said fretfully. 'How is the driver? I remember him swearing, so I know he's not badly hurt.'

'He's not hurt at all,' Max said crisply. 'Unlike you, he's aware of road safety—he was wearing his seat belt.' His tone altered. 'Apart from your head, how does the rest of you feel?'

'Battered,' she admitted. 'But truly, there's not much wrong. Can you apologise to the driver for me? I must have scared him witless.'

'You did. He's down in the hall being interrogated by the local police, and hugely relieved that he hasn't killed you.'

Her smile was pale and transitory. 'I feel so silly,' she said. 'How was your day?'

'Good.' He put her hand back on the coverlet. 'The doctor is glowering at me from the door so I'd better go. Do what he and the nurse tell you. Just take it easy—try to sleep.'

'Not much chance of doing anything else.' She sighed, then winced. 'I know it was stupid, and now I've just made things more difficult for you. Sorry, Max.'

'You should be.' He stooped and kissed her

on the forehead—like a father kissing his child, but even that chaste salute brought heat to her cheeks.

'Don't worry about anything,' he commanded, and was gone.

Next morning her headache had vanished, but the bruises she'd felt the night before had begun to appear in all their glory. Not only were they an interesting blue, but they hurt whenever she moved—even when she breathed.

When the doctor paid his morning visit, Max asked the doctor curtly, 'Is it possible she's broken a rib?'

The doctor shook his head. 'She hasn't even cracked one—she'd be in much more discomfort if she had. It's just the bruises. It will be some days before she feels comfortable again.'

'I'm here,' Rosa said crisply. 'And conscious.' She glared at them both. 'And there's nothing wrong with my ribs—I've had a cracked rib, and, believe me, this is nothing like that.'

'When did you crack a rib?' Max asked.

'Falling off a horse when I was sixteen.' Mortified, she wondered what on earth had made her let that out. Defiantly, she went on, 'At our villa on the royal island. Just after you left, if I remember correctly.'

Of course she remembered everything, especially embarrassing him with her unwanted adoration. She'd fallen because she'd been weeping at Max's departure with his gorgeous, charming girlfriend, and her horse had stumbled.

He lifted a black brow. 'I didn't hear about that,' he said, his voice completely neutral.

'Why would you?' Cheeks slightly flushed, she said to the doctor, 'I need to get up as soon as I can.'

'Not today.' He and Max spoke together.

Deferring to superior knowledge, Max gestured the doctor to go on.

'This morning you stay in bed,' the older man said sternly. 'This afternoon if you feel like it you can sit in a chair for an hour or so. Tomorrow, spend the morning in the chair and in the afternoon take a short gentle walk around the room. Gradually work up to a full day on your feet. You'll feel those bruises until they fade.'

Rosa's jaw jutted. 'I have to get up today. I have work to do.'

Max said authoritatively, 'She'll stay in bed.'

So Rosa waited until they were both gone to push back the bedclothes and swing her legs over the side. Muscles she didn't even know she had protested in outrage and beads of sweat broke out on her forehead, but she clenched her teeth and grabbed the head of the bed, using it to lever herself upwards.

'What are you doing?' The nurse rushed across to the bed. 'Highness, it won't do you any good to force yourself to get up. What will the prince say?'

'Plenty, no doubt,' Rosa said, swaying slightly, but already feeling better for being on her feet. Max would be only too pleased to see the back of her, so the sooner she got up and moving, the better.

The nurse looked torn. 'I shall tell him,' she decided, and turned to the door.

'No!' But Rosa's command was overlaid by another voice, cold and uncompromising.

'Get into that bed,' Max said, and when she stared mutinously at him, hiding the heady clamour his arrival caused, he strode across the room, picked her up with a strength that couldn't be denied, and with exquisite care eased her back under the covers.

'And this time, stay there!' he commanded, the steely note in his voice even more intimidating than his expression.

Tactfully, the nurse disappeared.

Before he had a chance to straighten up, Rosa said quietly, 'Do you know what to do with the vines?'

He was so close she could see the fine grain of his skin across his cheekbones, and recall with abrupt and intense accuracy how it had felt beneath her fingertips.

Perhaps something of that forbidden delight surfaced in her eyes, because Max stood up abruptly and took a pace back from the side of the bed. 'No. But no one will expect you to do anything when you're hurt.'

'*You'd* ignore the pain and get back to work,' she charged.

'That's different.'

She shrugged. 'So much for equality of the sexes.'

'Men are stronger than women.' He held up an imperative hand when she opened her mouth to refute that. Amusement gleamed in his eyes. 'Yes, I know scientists have proved that when it comes to endurance women last longer, but there's no need for you to endure anything. I've spoken to the lab staff; they're certain they know what to look for now, but it would help if you could write out that protocol for checking the vines, and another for the tests they need to do if any more outbreaks are suspected. Make both as detailed as you can.'

Rosa hated to give in, but, with every muscle in her body wrenched and aching, she accepted that for at least while she worked on the protocols she could stay in bed. 'All right,' she said coolly.

He looked down at her with narrowed eyes. 'Can I trust you to stay in bed?'

She was going to object, but something stayed her tongue. He had enough to worry about; the only way she could ease his burden was do as he asked. 'Yes,' she said, adding, 'For today, anyway.'

Although his frown warned her that he wasn't impressed, she went on steadily, 'Tomorrow I'll see how I feel, but staying in bed isn't going to help my bruises. And I need to supervise the monitoring of the vines.'

His eyes narrowed. 'Another thing I didn't realise was how obstinate you are. Yesterday you showed the technicians how to do that.'

'They need overseeing.' Her smile was a warning. 'As for obstinacy, how do you think I managed to persuade my parents to let me take my scientific bent seriously? Both of them—but my mother especially—wanted a completely different life for me.'

Max walked across to the window, standing there and staring out over the town and the valley. Rosa let her eyes feast greedily on his tall form, dominating the room against the blue, blue sky of summer. In spite of her efforts to control and subdue it, the swift kick of arousal was always there, even though she knew it could never be appeased.

Finally he turned and said austerely, 'It seems there is no end to the sacrifices Niroli requires of us. Very well. Tomorrow you can do what you feel is necessary, but today you stay in bed.'

So she did, working on step-by-step instructions, making them as clear and positive as she could.

That night Max read the results of her efforts in his office, then handed the papers over to Giovanni. 'What do you think?'

The older man perused them, finally pronouncing, 'Excellent. She has a clear and logical mind, the princess, and with this to refer to and tick off, surely no one can miss even the smallest sign of trouble.'

'I'll get my PA to organise for them to be printed and laminated, and we'll make sure every household has at least one copy.'

Nodding, Giovanni put the paper down on the desk. He hesitated, then said casually, 'She has grown into a charming woman.'

'She has,' Max said, and got to his feet. 'Stubborn, also. Tomorrow she insists on getting up.'

Giovanni smiled, but his dark eyes were troubled. 'You call it stubborn,' he chided, 'but most would say it's strength of character. Besides, some have made the same accusation about you.'

Shrugging, Max said, 'A family trait, then. Now, I suggest we go to bed early tonight, as tomorrow looks like being a long day.'

'Look, a perfect morning,' the nurse said, flinging back the curtains. 'One for the gods. How do you feel after a night's sleep?'

'Much better,' Rosa told her firmly. 'Well enough to get up.'

Tut-tutting, the nurse helped her to dress, suggesting that for today no bra was necessary.

'Not that you need one,' she observed, easing a soft silk shirt over Rosa's shoulders. 'You have a model's figure—slim and elegant.'

Rosa, who for years had envied her sister her more voluptuous body, smiled with a hint of irony and tried not to flinch as she got into a pair of loose trousers. 'It would have been nice to know what was in my future when I was growing up all gawky and awkward.'

The nurse chuckled. 'Ah, you would have found something else to worry about! Teenagers always do.'

Like falling in love with a forbidden man? She'd wanted so desperately to be beautiful like Isabella, because then Max might see something in her.

And now it didn't matter; the family rule she'd barely thought of in her teens stood like a wall between them. Until the death of her parents they could have married. Oh, it would have caused a scandal and cut both of them out of the succession, but it would have been possible.

Now it wasn't. Max's conscience wouldn't allow it.

Neither would hers. Even if he loved her she couldn't lure him into a relationship. He was the ruler Niroli needed to coax it into the twenty-first century.

Biting her lip, because her body was letting her know in no uncertain terms that it resented any movement, she pulled on her boots.

Someone knocked on the door. Her heart picked up speed, accelerating even further when the door opened to reveal a very grim Max. 'Is anything wrong?'

'Only that you're insisting on this,' he said curtly, coming into the room. 'Ready?'

'Yes,' she said with emphasis, only to spoil it by wincing when she took the first step.

'Get back into bed,' Max said lethally.

Her head came up. 'No.'

Their eyes duelled across the room. Finally Max shrugged. 'On your own head be it. I'll carry you down.'

'No,' she said, both excited and appalled. 'I'm too heavy.'

He looked at her with glittering eyes. 'In that case, you won't be able to make your way down the stairs. And even if did you crawl down them on stubborn will-power alone, after that you won't be fit to do any sort of supervision, let alone a whole day of it.' He paused, before saying deliberately, 'I won't drop you.'

He didn't want to do it, she could tell, but he was right. Bracing herself for his touch, she said, 'You'd better install elevators.'

'Why?' Gently he scooped her up and turned towards the door. 'You'll be leaving soon, and no one else has ever needed them.'

'Oh, rub it in,' she grumbled, because her body was purring into life, sensuous and catlike now that she was in his arms. 'I know I used to trip over a lot, but, truly, until I came back to Niroli I thought I'd outgrown my clumsiness.'

'You're not clumsy—you never were. Even when you were growing so fast you had trouble controlling your long limbs, you reminded me of a colt, all arms and legs but with the promise of grace and elegance,' he said, negotiating the stairs with steady confidence. 'I used to wonder how you could see through that mane of hair.'

And why her mother hadn't persuaded her into having it cut, he remembered. Although his aunt Francesca had loved both her daughters, she'd had much more in common with Isabella. She simply hadn't known how to deal with a forth-right, determined kid with a passion for such unfashionable interests as biology and science.

Uncannily echoing his thoughts, Rosa said, 'You gave me my first microscope when I was eight.'

He smiled. 'I'm surprised it stayed in your memory.'

She'd stammered her thanks, later confiding shyly that it was the best present she'd ever had, even better than her pony. She'd been such a straightforward child, speaking her mind with sometimes alarming results. Time, he thought, hefting his fragrant armful a little higher as he eased down the final few stairs, hadn't changed her much, although she'd learned circumspection.

His body stirred, its uncivilised impulses barely curbed by consideration and the fear of hurting her further. 'How the hell did you manage to walk into poor old Gesemane's car?'

'He hadn't bothered to switch on his lights,' she said in self-defence. 'But I was thinking of something else.'

'Trying to work out what to do for the vines?'

When she nodded her hair brushed his cheek, silky and warm, scented with some faint perfume that set his body onto full alert.

'I suppose I must have been,' she said, not exactly evading an answer.

Max wondered what she wasn't telling him. 'Promise me you'll take it easy today, and stop when you start to feel tired.'

'Don't nag,' she said spiritedly. 'I'm not stupid. I don't want to be a bother to you, so I'll give up when I have to.'

They'd reached the bottom of the stairs. Mysterious, exotic eyes flicked a glance his way. 'Put me down now, please.'

Without stopping he said, 'Are you sure?'

'Yes.' Her voice was strained. 'Put me down, Max.'

It was a relief to set her on her feet. 'Show me that you can walk,' he commanded.

Ready to snatch her back, he watched closely as she moved, at first stiffly and slowly, grimacing once when she straightened, but her head came up and she said gallantly, 'I'm fine. I'm not going to be the fastest person on the street, but I'll manage.'

'A walking stick will help,' Max said. He gave an order to the hovering manservant.

A stick was the last thing she wanted, but after a few more steps she had to admit that he was right. Although the protests from her body eased slightly, she felt unbalanced and precarious, so with relief she accepted the stick produced by the servant.

'What a beauty!' Carved from some dark wood, it finished in a dragon's head made of amber, worn smooth by many hands. She examined it with interest.

'Never mind what it looks like, try it,' Max ordered.

Rosa obeyed, carefully at first and then with more assurance. 'It does make a difference.' With a fleeting, fascinating glance up from beneath her lashes, she murmured, 'I feel quite dashing.'

His eyes must have revealed something of his feelings, because she coloured and lifted her chin in mute defiance.

Reining in his overwhelming need to protect her from anything that might hurt her, he said lightly, 'Dashing? Yes, you look it too—but then you always do. Now, before we go—'

'We?' Excitement funnelled through Rosa like a gift from the old gods of the island, bringing more colour to her skin, and a fugitive smile. 'Why? Are you coming too? You don't need to—'

'Of course I am. I don't trust you—you'd keep going until you dropped, and no one else has the power to tell you what to do.'

'Neither do you,' she said sweetly.

His grin was swift and very buccaneering. 'But I can pick you up and carry you away.'

'Brute force is not in the least appealing,' she said, then stopped, chagrined as she realised she was flirting with him.

Detachment cooled his voice. 'I'm not trying to appeal to you. You're important to Niroli.'

Her lashes flickered as she acknowledged the hit. 'Of course,' she said evenly, straightening her back and shoulders to stride out into the sunlight.

CHAPTER SEVEN

ROSA spent that day with the team who'd oversee the monitoring after she left Niroli. She impressed on them why everything had to be done in a certain way, and why it was vital to keep records up to date, why double-checking any significant deviation from the norm was important.

Max stayed with her until mid-morning, when a call on his phone brought a frown to his face.

'A business emergency,' he told her curtly, snapping the tiny phone shut. He looked around. 'Giovanni, I have to hand over to you. Make sure the princess doesn't tire herself too much. If she does, you know how to find me.'

Chagrined, Rosa snorted, but her eager group of students grinned and some of the braver ones chorused that they'd monitor her as closely as they planned to check the vines.

Often during that long, hot day Rosa looked up to find Giovanni's gaze on her. Each time he smiled and looked away, seemingly without embarrassment.

At first she thought it might be that he, like his fellow islanders, found the existence of a woman in charge oddly dislocating. Later it occurred to her that somehow he might be suspicious of the relationship between her and Max. Hot with shame, she wondered if someone had seen that forbidden kiss. Her mother used to say that servants knew everything…

That night she insisted she could walk up the first flight of stairs. Crisply, Max said, 'Don't be an idiot, Rosa. You're exhausted. I'll carry you up.'

'Carrying me up will be harder than coming down.' A quick survey of his formidable expression persuaded her to try for a compromise. 'All right—I'll go as far as I can, and you can carry me from there.'

She met his hard green scrutiny with a level stare. For a second she thought she'd lost, until his shoulders lifted in an abrupt shrug. 'So. Try then.'

Relieved, she gritted her teeth and made it to

the landing before her legs finally informed her they weren't going any further. Stone-faced, Max picked her up and set off up the stairs.

Rosa kept her eyes fixed on the paintings up the staircase, an impressive collection of landscapes from the golden age of the eighteenth century. Halfway up she mustered her courage to ask, 'Why does Giovanni watch me?'

Max's frown was obvious in his tone. 'I don't know.'

So he'd noticed it too. In a low, troubled voice she said, 'You don't think that anyone saw us— the other night?'

'No one saw it.' This time his tone was even yet forbidding. 'Giovanni knows me very well. He may suspect, that's all.'

Alarmed, she caught her upper lip in her teeth. He didn't look at her, and she didn't take him up on the final sentence. Eventually she said, 'I'll leave as soon as I can. I just hope no more vine-yards are affected.'

Was it her imagination, or did his arms tighten around her? At the top of the stairs she said, 'Put me down, please.'

He didn't object. Once on her feet she looked

up and saw a gleam of sweat across his forehead. 'I told you it would be too much,' she said accusingly. 'I hope I haven't given you a hernia!'

Max threw his head back and laughed, and after a moment she laughed too, unwillingly compelled by the personal magnetism that gave him such presence.

'No hernia,' he said. 'Good night, Rosa. Sleep well.'

'You too,' she said quietly.

He gave her a smile so impregnated with irony that it hurt. 'The important thing is for you to rest. Oh—Maria the maid says she has some special ointment that her grandmother heartily recommends for bruising. She'd like to massage you, if you want her to.'

Without heat Rosa said, 'I'm sure you've already discussed it with the doctor.'

'He thinks it an excellent idea,' he told her smoothly. 'And Maria assures me she has gentle hands. She's worked at the spa on the south coast, so she should know what to do, but if you find her too rough I'll get one of the masseuses from the spa here.'

'I'll try anything if it helps.'

'So that you can get away sooner?' he said with a twisted smile, and left her staring after him.

Rosa woke in the early dawn, and gave a few exploratory stretches. The maid had promised her that the herb-scented cream she'd used to rub her down would work like a miracle from the saints. She'd been right; although the bruises were now spectacular, the deep-seated ache had gone, and if she moved cautiously there was almost no pain.

'Someone should patent it,' Rosa murmured, climbing cautiously out of the bed. Perhaps the spa on the south coast would like to hear about it...

Whatever, she felt almost human this morning.

For the next two weeks Max divided his time between Cattina and the capital, with one foray to a high-powered business meeting in Geneva that kept him away overnight. When he was home, Rosa made first her bruises, and when they'd faded the reports she was writing to New Zealand, an excuse for retiring to her bedroom immediately after dinner—acutely aware of his relief, well-hidden though it was.

At least she was now feeling fine. The doctor was pleased when at Max's insistence he visited her one last time.

'You're young and strong,' he informed her. 'And you have no bad habits. Naturally you heal fast.'

'So when will I be able to fly back to New Zealand?'

His satisfied smile transmuted into a frown. 'I certainly wouldn't advise that. You feel well now, but the body is a delicate instrument, and so many hours cooped up…' He shook his head. 'Wait a week—better yet, two.' And when she opened her mouth to protest he added with the air of one who knew he had a clincher, 'I am sure the prince would agree with me.'

Max did. 'I'll send you back in the private jet,' he said when she raised the point after dinner that night. 'But not for another ten days. Dr Fiorelli was very definite.'

'Whatever happened to patient/doctor confidentiality?' she demanded, incensed.

'Apparently he feels it's superseded by his duty to his patient,' he shot back, eyes green and implacable. 'So do I. And had you forgotten that your boss wants you here until at least the end of the month to report progress?'

'I hadn't.' She looked down at her hands, ruthlessly shutting off the part of her brain that kept obsessing over how addictive he was. Clearly she was doomed to stay here until Max decided she could go.

Rosa didn't try to change his mind; she knew her limitations. Switching tack, she said, 'I hope—I *think*—I've managed to impress on everyone concerned the need for absolute regularity and impeccable record-keeping.'

'You have,' he said with a confidence that warmed some vulnerable part of her. 'They might seem a bit casual, but they know how much depends on this.'

'And Giovanni says he'll keep a very close watch on them.' She hesitated, some hidden superstitious part of her wondering if her next words were tempting fate. 'At least it doesn't look as though there are going to be any further outbreaks.'

'With any luck we've got it under control.' He walked across to the drinks tray. 'Would you like a drink before you go to bed?'

'No, thank you.' Since the night he'd given her brandy she'd allowed herself nothing more than a glass of wine with dinner. Anything else might weaken her will-power, already incredibly fragile where Max was concerned.

She went on, 'But it's only a stopgap measure, Max. We—or some other research centre—will eventually find a cure, or a way to stop transmission that doesn't involve such brutal measures as burning every vine. Until then we can only do what we already have done. And hope.'

'It's called buying time, and, in a situation like this, sometimes it's the only thing left to do.' He smiled at her, his expression softening. 'Having seen you work here, I'm sure you'll come up with something. You have great dedication.'

The compliment brought a rush of colour to her cheeks. Hoarding it to the tiny cupboard in her mind where his other compliments had been stored, she said, 'We will.' But honesty compelled her to add, 'If it's at all possible.'

'And if it's not possible, we'll have to learn to live with it.'

His words sounded flat and ominous. Rosa flinched, then told herself she'd have to stop connecting everything he said with the tension that had been building between them since she'd come back to Niroli.

She looked down at her hands, their long fingers entwined in her lap. 'Before I go I want to visit my parents' grave on Royal Island—just for an hour or so. And when I see Grandpapa in Porto Di Castellante I'd like to call on your mother.'

'An excellent idea, but unfortunately she's still in France. Do you have friends in the capital?'

'Not really,' she confessed with reluctance.

The children she'd known on Niroli had been the sons and daughters of the aristocracy, chosen by her mother, with each encounter supervised by her governess. Her enduring friendships had been made at the school in Switzerland and at university.

'Poor lonely little princess,' Max said softly.

She gave him a sharp look, expecting to see mockery gleaming in his eyes. Instead, she saw a shadow of tenderness that stabbed her to the heart.

Ever since their explosive kiss they'd been so careful not to cross that forbidden boundary. Their restraint should have worked to ease the situation. It hadn't; Rosa felt as though she were walking a tightrope, each long day increasing the unspoken tension between her and Max until her every nerve was on edge, charged with feverish, forbidden anticipation.

Curtly she said, 'I'm not poor, and I'm certainly not lonely. I'd go to Mont Avellana to stay with Isabella and Domenic, only I want to be close to Cattina in case something else develops here.'

'Why don't you finish recuperating on Royal Island?' Max watched her with eyes shaded by long lashes. 'You'll be well looked after at your family villa.'

Rosa said unevenly, 'I don't know—I haven't stayed there since Mamma and Papà were... died.'

After a moment's taut silence he came across to crouch beside her chair and take her hands in his. 'You should go back, Rosa. Although their death was tragic, they would not have wanted you to grieve for ever.'

If he came with her she could bear it, she thought, but of course he wouldn't.

Couldn't.

Playing with fire had never been her favourite way of entertaining herself either. Swallowing the lump in her throat, she conceded bleakly, 'I know, but—'

He interrupted, 'You need to face the ghosts.'

'There are no ghosts,' she protested. 'We were always so happy on the island.'

'The ghosts of the happy past are sometimes harder to face than unhappiness,' he said quietly.

His understanding pierced her heart. If she looked up she'd see the tiny nerve flicking in his jaw, but keeping her eyes fixed on their linked hands was another, more subtle torture. His touch was warm and secure. If only it could be like this…

Someone coughed from the door.

Max got to his feet in a rapid, almost abrupt movement, and said in a voice totally without inflection, 'Giovanni. What has brought you here?'

Rosa eased out of the chair. 'I'll leave you to talk alone.'

'It is about the vines,' Giovanni said.

Rosa froze, and looked up at Max. His face had hardened; in a voice like a whip-crack he said, 'Tell me, man!'

With a troubled glance at Rosa, Giovanni said, 'It looks like another outbreak.'

'Dear God,' Max said in a voice that sent chills down Rosa's spine. 'Where?'

'Next door to one of the vineyards we've just treated for the blight.'

Max said harshly, 'And thank God for that. At least it's not a new outbreak. So the vines will have been drenched with the disinfectant?'

'Yes,' Giovanni said.

Max looked at Rosa. 'Could this be a reaction to the spray?'

With all her heart, Rosa wished she could say yes, but she shook her head. 'It doesn't seem likely,' she said slowly, her mind racing to recall all the information she had. 'None of the test vines showed any reaction, but I can't say it's impossible. If you'll wait a few minutes I'll just change my clothes—'

'There's no need for you to go out.' Max's expression was forbidding. 'You have done what you came to Niroli to do—given us hope. Now you must let us work on it. Go up to bed.'

'I am not a servant—' she began heatedly, falling silent when she met his eyes.

Hard and cold and completely intimidating, they gave no quarter. 'Show the people you have trained that you trust them.'

She narrowed her gaze. 'You're a manipulative devil,' she said jaggedly, but her tone told him he'd won.

The eastern sky was a soft dove-grey when Max drove into the castello forecourt. Beside him Giovanni sat in silence, his brows drawn together as though dealing with unpleasant thoughts.

Max glanced at him. He looked old, he thought, and weary, but that was to be expected. He felt old and weary himself. At least it wasn't another outbreak! Rosa's checklist had proved conclusively that the vineyard was clear of shot blight; the holes had been chewed by insects. In fact there was a lot to be pleased about; one of the vineyard hands had reported the possible outbreak, so clearly the message was getting through to everyone.

But he sensed that something else was worrying the man who had been more than a father to him than his own had ever been.

'Come inside and we'll have a drink to warm

our hearts,' he said. 'Then you can go home and sleep. You've been working long hours, and it's showing. I don't want to see you again before tomorrow morning. What you really need is to spend a couple of days sitting in the sun and talking about anything but vines. When this is over, old friend, we'll both do that.'

Although Giovanni smiled, his heart wasn't in it. 'Not you—you have other responsibilities. And thank you, I will come in, even though I am dirty.'

'I'm just as dirty as you are,' Max told him wryly.

In the study Giovanni watched Max poured two small glasses of the island's potent brandy. He held one out to him, saying, 'Sit down, and drink this—it will warm you, and give you heart before you go home to bed.'

But Giovanni stayed standing, looking down into the small glass where the amber liquid shifted slightly. His hands were trembling, Max realised, and he felt a sudden stab of compunction. This situation had been difficult for them all, but Giovanni had taken it harder than most.

Rosa's faint perfume drifted tantalisingly in the air. Max suspected that he'd never be able to rid the castello of that fragrance; it was one of the happy ghosts, he thought, then chided himself for being morbid. Soon the castello would no longer be his home.

Once in the palace, he'd eventually be able to wall off the bitter ache that was his feelings for her.

Uneasily, Max watched as his companion, normally almost abstemious, tossed the brandy down his throat in one swallow. 'Sit, man,' he said.

'I'll stand.' Giovanni looked around him, avoiding Max's scrutiny. 'I wish to speak to you—one man to another.'

Max frowned. 'Have we not always spoken—one man to another?' he said. 'Or have I been mistaken these many years?'

'No, you have not been mistaken, but when one man carries a secret in his heart, there is not complete frankness. I must ask you—do you love the Princess Rosa?'

Max felt his face stiffen into an austere mask. He didn't answer for a long time, but Giovanni waited, obviously tense but not giving in. He looked old and grey, as though faced with an agonising decision. Or death.

'Why are you asking this?'

Giovanni said patiently, 'I know that you feel something for her.'

'So?' Max demanded.

'But it does not seem to me that you are yet lovers.'

Max's eyes narrowed. 'It isn't possible, as you well know. The family rules forbid it.'

Giovanni studied his face for an intent few moments. 'If I told you it was possible,' he said heavily, 'would you marry her?'

'What is this?' Max demanded, reining in a sudden anger. 'We are cousins—first cousins! Our fathers were half-brothers. The rules of the royal house say that it is not possible for blood relations to marry.'

Giovanni said, 'I think I will sit down after all.'

Max said swiftly, 'So, sit.' He helped the elderly man into a chair—the one that Rosa usually sat in. 'You do not look well. I'll call the doctor.'

'No,' Giovanni said. He dragged in a breath and went on, pausing between the words as though each one hurt. 'You and the princess are not cousins. There is no blood connection between you. Your father was not the king's son.'

Any other man Max would have knocked to the ground, but this man was known over the whole island for his integrity. In all the years he'd known him, Max had never heard him lie.

Mind working furiously, he said, 'You're saying that my grandmother—Queen Eva—wasn't faithful to my...to the king.'

Giovanni closed his eyes. 'That is so.'

'Then who was my grandfather?'

Another long silence, until Giovanni said in a deeply shamed voice, 'I am.'

Max picked up his brandy and drank half of it down in a gulp. With the liquid burning his stomach, he asked icily, 'And how do you know this? Birth dates are notoriously difficult to link to the act that causes them.'

'I don't blame you for finding it difficult to believe,' Giovanni said, his voice trembling. 'I don't know that the queen knows herself, and the king obviously doesn't because he accepted your father as his son.' He hesitated before finishing starkly, 'Although I think he suspects.'

'Then why are you so certain?' Max demanded.

In answer Giovanni pulled a photograph out of his pocket and held it out. 'This,' he said succinctly.

For the second time in his life, Max didn't want to face what lay ahead of him. He had to force himself to take the few steps to take the photograph, and then to look at it.

An old photograph of a young man, smiling at the lens.

At first he thought it was a photograph of himself, taken when he was eighteen or nineteen, but almost immediately discarded that idea. The clothes were wrong, and he'd never owned a motorcycle.

'Who is this?' Each word was clear and cold and short.

'My younger brother, Vittorio,' Giovanni said and crossed himself reverently. 'Our mother was English; she met my father when he was in England working for an uncle, a wine-seller in London. They married, but she could never settle here, and when Vittorio was only five she went back to England and divorced my father there. We never saw my brother again—when he was nineteen he was killed on that motorcycle. Our mother sent this photograph back just before it happened. She died shortly after him.'

Max said nothing, searching the face in the

photograph. At some cell-deep level he sensed that, not only was Giovanni telling the truth, but that the old man in front of him was his true grandfather.

'I first saw you when you were three, and I knew then,' Giovanni said. He shook his head. 'Your father looked like the queen, his mother, but you—you were Vittorio all over again. I wondered whether I should tell anyone, but it seemed that nothing needed to be done, because who would have thought that your cousins and your brothers would refuse the throne?'

Max fought back a cold fury. 'You'd have let me ascend it, knowing I had no right to it?'

Giovanni shrugged. 'You are a good man,' he said simply. 'You know the islanders, you have worked hard for them, and you have been successful in the world also. What better man could be our king?'

'So why…?' He stopped, because he knew why. 'Rosa,' he said harshly. 'Is it that obvious?'

'No!' Giovanni stared at him. 'I—know you well. When she came back, I saw that you wanted her. And because you have the sort of integrity that makes everyone uncomfortable, I knew that you would send her away. And I could not bear that. I have loved you ever since I saw you. I have thought long and hard about this, and it seems to me that I cannot make you suffer because of a lie.'

Max finished off the rest of the brandy, welcoming its smooth heat, waiting for its warmth. None came. 'I see. But although it's true that if Rosa and I are not related we could marry—if we decided it was what we want—*she* will still be bound by the rules. The first one, if you remember, is that no member of the royal family can be joined in marriage without the consent and approval of the ruler. If you think the king will give his consent for her to marry me—the product of an adulterous liaison of his wife—then I can tell you you're wrong.'

Testily Giovanni countered, 'There is no need for scandal! Why stir up mud when it's not necessary? Let things go on as they are, achieve the throne and then as King you can amend the rule to something a little less severe.'

Of course Giovanni, pragmatic to the core, would think that a perfectly feasible way to deal with this situation!

Max fought temptation, seductive and sweet as honey. Harshly he said, 'I don't know if I'd be able to change the rules, but, even if I could, to marry Rosa without scandal is impossible. All my life I have been brought up to respect the monarchy and the people of Niroli. I can't change now.'

Watching Giovanni—his *grandfather*!—get to his feet, he said abruptly, 'But whatever I do, know this—I could not have had a better grandfather.'

Giovanni's eyes filled with tears. 'Nor I a better grandson,' he said, and hauled Max into his arms for a fierce, quick hug.

When it was over they looked at each other with some embarrassment, a moment ended when Giovanni said, 'I shall go now. But remember what I have always told you—don't do anything in a hurry. Decisions made when the emotions run hot are always bad.' He paused, then said with a brave attempt at a smile, 'Such as the one that eventually led to your birth. But I was young and easily impressed by beauty. And how can I regret it when I have such a grandson?'

That was all very well, Max thought after he'd taken the old man home, but what the hell was he going to do now?

And more to the point—should he tell Rosa? Mind in turmoil, he walked across to his bedroom window and stared out at the vines, line upon line of them stretching along the riverside and up to braid the foothills, precious beyond belief.

He'd reconciled himself to selling up his financial and commercial interests, and to loosening his hands on the reins here, but he'd assumed that as King he'd be able to watch over the industry. The castello would always be his; it had come to him through Queen Eva's father, a nobleman of the island, but after Giovanni's astounding revelation he'd have to tell the old king that he couldn't take the throne.

And that, he thought wearily, would almost certainly mean a voluntary exile from Niroli, while the king worked his way through the constitutional crisis that would follow.

The sun leapt above the horizon, gilding the valley and the mountains as a chorus of cocks around the city welcomed it with a full-throated chorus. Max's involuntary smile faded.

He couldn't go to the king without proof. The old man wouldn't accept a photograph, so that meant DNA testing. He frowned. That would take about six weeks.

No, there must be a way to hurry things along. He remembered a court case that rested on such tests; they had been completed in a week.

But if it proved that Giovanni's story was correct, Rosa was the only person left to ascend the throne.

CHAPTER EIGHT

MAX'S hands tightened into fists. The people of
Niroli—most of them salt-of-the-earth peasants
with a strong attachment to tradition—would
find it difficult to accept a reigning queen.

And Rosa would hate it. As she'd probably
hate being Queen Consort, he reminded himself
with brutal honesty.

Of course, he could be wildly off the mark
thinking that he'd seen love in her eyes and not
just a passionate attachment with sexual satisfaction as its only aim.

Disconnected thoughts tumbling through his
brain, he stood there, watching the light bring the
soft colours of a Mediterranean autumn to life,
the sounds and smells and warmth. A massive
yawn took him by surprise.

'Four hours' sleep,' he said grimly, alerting the
clock in his brain, and went to bed.

* * *

Rosa spent the morning in the vineyard. When the sun strode up to its zenith in the burning sky she straightened up and asked the three technicians who'd been helping, 'What do you think?'

After a startled moment the boldest said, 'Nothing. They're all clear—it's definitely insect infestation, not shot blight.'

'OK, tell me what you base that decision on.'

He told her, the others nodding agreement, but when he'd finished they looked somewhat anxiously at her.

Grinning, she said, 'You're dead right. They're clear as a bell.' She waited until their excited whoops died down before cautioning, 'Not that you can relax. You'll need to keep checking every vine, every week until the outbreak is only a memory.'

'When will that be?' a quiet, serious young woman asked.

'Six months,' she said soberly. 'But after that there should be monthly checks. Once shot blight has appeared anywhere, it tends to recur at irregular intervals. Eternal vigilance is necessary.'

One of them, a young man fresh out of university, ventured, 'Some of the peasants say we're overdoing the destruction of the vines.'

'I know,' she said to murmurs of assent. 'What do you think?'

She watched keenly as they replied, especially a young woman who'd argued previously that it might be better to wait and see rather than risk antagonising the vineyard owners with such drastic measures.

'She still believes that,' she told Max later as they ate lunch at the castello.

'What's her name?' When she'd told him, he nodded. 'She has roots deep in Cattina—of course she sympathises with the growers. However I'll have her taken off the assessment team.'

Rosa said in a troubled voice, 'I understand that you know these people well, but are you positive that's the best way to tackle it?'

'I'll make sure she has an equivalent position where she can't hamper the on going surveillance,' he said, a note of ruthless determination tempering his voice. 'If she isn't committed she may be tempted to leave someone's vineyard just one more day to see what happens.'

'And that could be fatal,' Rosa agreed. But after a moment's consideration she added, 'She's good, though, with an excellent degree from

Italy. Is there a system here to pick out talent and send them for further study?'

Max surveyed her keenly. 'No. Do you think she's worth it?'

'I do.'

'I'll put someone onto it. One of the things I'm going to make sure of is that…' The pause was so slight Rosa almost missed it. Barely missing a beat, he finished on a bland note, 'Niroli needs a formal process and funding to search out these excellent students and sponsor them for further education. We can't afford to waste talent.'

What had he been planning to say? Rosa's lashes drooped. Max was…different, somehow. Not merely aloof and withdrawn, as he had been after that searing kiss, but guarded.

Or was she fantasising?

He went on, 'You're too fine-drawn, and those tilted eyes have shadows. Now that you're confident you've trained your people to interpret any signs of shot blight, a few days at the villa with nothing more to do than swim and laze in the sun will set you up for the trip home.'

One swift glance from beneath her lashes

showed that he had no intention of accompanying her. He just wanted to get rid of her. That odd sound must be the noise of forlorn hope splintering, she thought wearily.

She tried to infuse her voice with calm composure. 'I've been thinking of that, and you were right—if I don't visit my parents' grave soon it will get more and more difficult to go back. And a few days there will give me time to collect my thoughts about the outbreak for the final report.'

Final only if no further outbreaks happened, of course.

Once the decision was made Max moved swiftly. Early next morning she left for the island, the ancient personal domain of the Niroli ruling family. From that fiefdom a bold, ruthless Fierezza ancestor had launched the power bid that brought him the throne; still fiercely loyal, the islanders always gave the royal family the privacy they needed.

Her arrival at the villa was every bit as traumatic as she'd feared. Although she fought to control her feelings, her eyes filled with tears when the housekeeper and maids greeted her.

One of the maids began to cry, and to Rosa's horror she couldn't hold back her own grief.

Clucking sympathetically, the housekeeper embraced her in motherly arms, patting her back until she hiccupped back the sobs.

'I'll make you a soothing tea,' she said, shooing the maids away. And when Rosa had washed her face and drunk the herb and honey concoction the older woman made, they talked about her parents and the happy holidays they'd spent there.

'At least they went together,' the housekeeper said pragmatically. 'They wouldn't have liked being separated, those two.' She sighed, and then brightened. 'They'd be glad to know you've come back.'

But Rosa couldn't persuade herself to visit their grave. Her flight to the island had been sheer self-protection; staying with Max had turned into irresistible torture, and for his sake and her own she had to get away.

For the next few days she dutifully swam and slowly polished her tan. In the mornings she collated the notes on her laptop, sending copies to Max by email.

His replies were reassuring—no new outbreaks, even the dissidents amongst the growers had settled down to a simmer, and the young woman who'd raised objections to the strict and rigorous regime was happily planning an academic year in a prestigious university in America.

The messages were short to the point of curtness, without any echo of sentiment—yet Rosa pored over each one and couldn't delete them. Working beside Max had transformed the remnants of a childish crush into something much more vigorous and dangerous.

She should never have come back to Niroli. But she couldn't have turned her back on the vine-growers' plight.

Rebellion ate into her. The stupid rules—drawn up in days when the king was an autocrat who needed to control his relatives in case they deposed him—still stood above the law of the land.

She snapped shut the book she'd been trying to read, and stared out to where the Mediterranean slept, blue and calm, the smallest of waves breathing gently onto the hot sand. The sun beat down on her, tenderly gilding skin exposed by skimpy shorts and a bra top, but for once she didn't relish its heat. Her grandfather must realise what those rules had cost him—heir after heir had given up their right to the throne rather than obey their strictures.

But Max wouldn't. She'd seen how deeply duty was ingrained in his personality; he'd sacrifice his life for the people of Niroli.

And of course, she thought bleakly, she had no idea what he felt for her. Passion, yes, but people could feel passion for lovers they didn't even like. Her angst and misery were useless and unprofitable, as well as being heavily larded with self-pity.

In spite of the languorous heat, she shivered. There was no hope for her.

So she'd have to find some way to get over this forbidden love, because it was doomed. In time she might even come to accept her loss with a sense of resignation—

'Rosa?'

Shocked delight fountained through her. She turned her head and saw him, a dark, forbidding figure beneath the pergola, his face shaded by the bougainvillea.

Her throat worked; she swallowed, but her

voice was still uneven. 'What—what are you doing here?'

His broad shoulders lifted fractionally and he came out into the sunlight. Rosa blinked.

He looked grim, the darkly arrogant features set as though he'd reached some decision, one that had cost him sleepless nights and a lot of painful thought.

But his voice was even and unemotional as he said, 'Everything's all right on Niroli. I just needed to see you before you go.'

With a small, smothered sound, she bolted up from the lounger and hurled herself into his arms.

Just once, she thought with a fierce determination to match his, she was going to know him in the most intimate, carnal sense. Although there could never be a future for them, there was the present. If anyone was going to take her virginity, she wanted it to be the man she'd loved and wanted for years.

'Oh, Max!' she said into his throat as his arms closed tightly around her. 'I've missed you.'

His voice—raw with unspoken hunger—filled her ears.

'I've missed you too,' he said, and then swore,

and when she lifted a startled face he gave a taut, mirthless smile and set her gently aside.

Humiliated by her own stupidity—flinging herself into his arms, for heaven's sake!—Rosa took refuge on the nearest lounger, sitting on it like a stool and folding her arms across her chest in a vain attempt to hide as much exposed golden skin as possible.

If only the furniture weren't so obviously made for sprawling. Why, oh, why hadn't she put on a shirt after her swim?

She flicked a glance at Max, who'd half turned away, no doubt giving her time to regain some composure.

'We have to talk,' he said in a level voice.

Chilled by the hard determination she glimpsed in his eyes, Rosa said as steadily as she could, 'About what?'

'First of all, there's a security expert checking the villa to make sure it's safe.'

'*Safe?*' Her voice rose on the word. 'What could be safer than the villa?'

He paused, choosing his words. 'Being dogged by paparazzi has made me paranoid—and there is a remote chance the villa's been bugged.'

Unease prickled though her skin, hollowed out her stomach. 'Why?' And why was he evading a straight answer to her question?

'According to the villagers at least one stranger has been snooping around trying to get them to talk about the family.'

'A British stranger?' she asked without thinking.

'Yes.' He shot her a penetrating glance. 'Have you seen anyone?'

'Possibly,' she said cautiously. 'The house-keeper told me about him. I think he took a photo of me in the village yesterday.'

He frowned. 'So he knows you're here, and by now he'll probably know I am too.' After another of those lightning-swift glances, he shrugged. 'Don't worry. The villa can't be overlooked unless he hires a helicopter, and he can't do that here.'

Then, with an abrupt change of subject, he said, 'You look much better. No sign of a bruise. Can you breathe without discomfort?'

'Yes, I'm fine. Max, what is it? You seem—different, somehow.'

Her words surprised a short, mirthless laugh from him. He sat down on a chair some little

distance away. 'Probably because I feel different. I need to tell you something.'

Rosa licked her lips, warned by something
subliminal in his attitude that she wasn't going
to like this. 'Go on,' she said hoarsely.

Without looking at her, he said calmly, 'It
appears that I—and my brothers—are not actually
the king's grandchildren.'

And as she gasped he went on to explain.

Appalled by the cool, measured words, Rosa
knew her face mirrored her changing emotions—
bewilderment, then stunned shock, followed by
horror when she realised where this revelation
was heading.

He finished by saying, 'I couldn't go to the
king with a photograph as the only evidence,
so Giovanni and I had DNA testing done. It
proved conclusively that he is my grandfather,
not the king.'

'I see,' she said in a small voice, looking down
at the hands that knotted in her lap. 'What—what
do you plan to do?'

'I'll tell the king.'

Rosa went cold, thinking of the proud, autocratic old man who was her grandfather. The

Fierezza blood meant everything to him. Colour faded from her smooth skin, leaving the framework prominent and angular. 'But there's no one else. What will he do?'

'He'll tell me to get the hell off Niroli and never come back.'

Stunned, she stared at him. His expression was unreadable, as emotionless as the bronze athlete he so resembled, but something in his steady tone struck her as false. She swallowed. 'Is that what you want? To leave Niroli?'

He shrugged. 'No. Strangely enough, I want to be King. There's a hell of a lot of work to be done here; Grandfather—the king,' he corrected himself with a harshly cynical twist to his lips, 'hasn't moved with the times. I think the islanders trust me. I'm certainly known to them. If I were King I could do an immense amount of good.' He paused, holding her gaze with his. 'But as I am not a Fierezza, that's no longer an option because of course the king won't allow anyone who's not a descendant to rule Niroli. He'll make you his heir.'

'No,' she whispered, shivering. She rubbed her hands up and down her upper arms in an attempt to warm them, then hugged herself in a childish, defensive gesture.

Mercilessly, Max said, 'There's only you left, Rosa.'

Shaking her head, she looked at him pleadingly, hoping he could produce another heir from behind his back like a magician. His handsome face—so like Giovanni's, she realised now—was coldly controlled.

'I know.' Her lips quivered. 'But will the people want to be ruled by a queen? There's never been one before and a lot of the islanders are very old-fashioned.'

'They'll accept you if there's no one else. You'll have to do it, Rosa.' He spoke ruthlessly, shattering all her faint, barely articulated dreams. 'If you don't, the republican party may well see it as a chance to push their agenda.'

She thought instantly of Kate's comments, so long ago it seemed now. 'Would that be such a bad thing?'

'Can you see them achieving it peacefully? Almost a generation ago Niroli was torn by a particularly bloody civil war—you lost a brother through it. You might have regained him, but

many others died. Rosa, you know the islanders—their memories are long and the royal
family is hugely important to them as a symbol,
if nothing else. They'll fight to retain the throne.'

He was already distancing himself, she
realised, shivering. His tone was quite dispassionate when he spoke of the royal house, as
though he'd already renounced any right to be
considered part of it.

Rosa closed her eyes and slumped while desperate thoughts whirled chaotically through her brain.
Fighting back, she seized on one and sat bolt
upright. 'What about Adam?'

When he looked impassively at her she
added hastily, 'You know Adam Ryder—my
half-brother.'

She was clutching at straws, and they both
knew it. 'He's your father's son, all right, but he's
illegitimate,' Max pointed out.

The light in her eyes died. She said passionately, 'It's so unfair! You'd make a terrific
king—the best we've ever had, probably. If it
turns out that Giovanni's right, couldn't you
keep quiet about your ancestry? Then you could
ascend the throne.'

'I'm no usurper,' he said with harsh distinctness. 'If I'm not a Fierezza I have no claim to the throne. Whatever happened, I wouldn't accept it.'

'Anyway, it won't change anything,' she said, her brow furrowing while her mind darted frantically around, settling on ideas only to discard them. 'Everyone would still believe we were cousins. Unless—'

Colour burning the length of her cheekbones, she stopped abruptly. Had he noticed? She stole a furtive look at him, but Max's expression hadn't altered. Perhaps he hadn't heard the implication in her words—that if she did accept the throne they could marry.

His face set in forbidding lines. 'As I'm not the king's grandson, there's going to be a huge scandal as well as a constitutional crisis. The tabloids will make an immense fuss about the queen's adultery, the king will be revealed to be a cuckolded husband—and you can imagine how that will go down with the islanders. Not only that, but my mother and brothers will be stripped of their titles. More food for the republicans.'

Rosa shivered at the wider implications of Giovanni's revelation.

Max said, 'Whereas if I simply announce that I don't want the throne, who'd be surprised? It isn't the first time, after all—every other heir has turned it down too.'

She sat in silence for some moments, digesting this, before she jerked upright, face clearing. 'No—*wait*! Couldn't Grandpapa legitimise Adam and let him rule Niroli?'

'I don't think it's possible.' He glanced at her and went on remorselessly, 'But even if Adam could be persuaded to accept the throne, do you think he'd give up his life in America?'

Rosa bit her lip. 'No. Why should he? He has no attachment to the island.' She felt sick and terrified, like a cornered animal being herded into a trap. She'd longed to know that she and Max weren't related—and her wish had been granted, but it only made things worse, more impossible than ever. The old proverb danced mockingly in her brain. *Be careful what you wish for—you might get it.*

A lump blocked her throat. She swallowed again, then said in a thin, desperate voice, 'There's no alternative, is there? I have to do it.'

'Duty is a bastard,' he said with flinty restraint.

She glanced at the bronze mask of his face. It revealed nothing. How had he felt when he realised that not only his life, but that of his father and brothers, had been based on a lie?

Forcing herself to ignore her own bleak apprehension, she said quietly, 'It must have been shattering to find out that you weren't who you thought you were.'

His expression altered too subtly for her to be able to read it. 'In a way it's a relief,' he said unexpectedly.

Rosa stared at him, and he gave a tigerish smile, leaned towards her and kissed her.

Sensation stormed through her in a wild clamour. It was like coming home again after years spent at sea, like finding the safe haven that had eluded her all her life. When he got to his feet and drew her up with him she gladly opened her mouth beneath the challenging demand of his.

Until he tore himself away and said in a voice she'd never heard before, his driven, desperate words searing her heart, 'I'm sorry. I promised myself that wouldn't happen.'

He let her go. Without looking at her he said harshly, 'I have no right to touch you.'

Faced by the possibility of an unbearable future, one devoted to duty and a responsibility she'd never wanted, never been trained for, one that would wrench her from her career and the life she enjoyed, Rosa cast prudence and any fear of rejection to the winds.

Fiercely she demanded, 'Do you know I'm still a virgin?'

Max froze, almost like a predator sensing prey, then turned his head slowly. Stone-faced except for the leaping gold lights in his eyes, he said, 'I wondered—but I couldn't believe you were.'

'Well, I am.' She ignored the whispered warnings of pride. 'And do you want to know why? I wanted you when I was sixteen, too young to understand what I felt, and I want you now. Max, make love to me.'

His face disciplined into that unreadable mask—beautiful, arrogant, enigmatic—he said only one word. 'Why?'

'Because I—' A little half-sob choked her, but she managed to quell her fear and collect herself enough to finish on a breathless, reckless rush, 'For purely selfish reasons. If we don't, I'll regret it all my life.'

How long they faced each other like enemies in the bright sunlight, her heart hammering so loudly it blocked out all other sounds, Rosa didn't know. It took every ounce of her courage to meet his steady, intimidating survey, and the challenging silence stretched between them, thick with unspoken thoughts.

Until he smiled.

Rosa fought back a primeval response that shrieked at her to run.

She swallowed. 'Max?'

Even then he didn't move. Instead his gaze fell from her eyes to her mouth, lingering there long enough for her lips to feel full and soft and heated.

Rosa held her head high, but when that green-gold survey skimmed her throat and the soft curves beneath, swift colour stung her skin, and to her astonishment and alarm her nipples budded into tight peaks.

'And if we make love,' he said on a raw note, 'you may regret that too.'

'No. Not that. Not ever.' It was like a vow and he frowned. He was going to say no, she knew it. Recklessly she blurted, 'If I have to be Queen

I need something—something of my own, something to remember, to warm me when I get cold at night…'

He paused, and she saw a flicker of compassion. With bitter resignation she accepted it, because he understood how she was feeling. Even though he wanted to help the people of Niroli, he'd never expected to be King.

'Are you sure, Rosa?'

'Utterly sure.'

He said, 'So be it, then,' and came towards her, his smile suddenly tender. 'I hope I don't hurt you. I've never made love to a virgin before.'

So it might even be special for him? 'You *couldn't* hurt me,' she said, no longer caring whether he loved her or not. The future stretched before her, shadowed by renunciation. She would at least have this.

Max lifted her chin with a forefinger, tilting her face to meet his. She flushed at the green flame in his hazel eyes, and he smiled, bent and kissed her for a fierce, passionate second, then picked her up and carried her across to the hammock suspended from the boughs of an ancient, evergreen tree that shaded the arbour.

In a dreamy, dazed voice she said, 'It's just as well the servants go home after breakfast—'

'—and won't come back until it's time to get dinner,' he finished for her, his eyes gleaming with a light she'd seen only once before.

Hardly able to believe it was going to happen, she shivered and gave him a tremulous smile. He didn't return it.

She said, 'I'm sorry. If you don't want to…' She stumbled to a halt and looked down, forming the words in her mind before she could say them. 'If you don't want to make love to me, then don't. It's all right.'

CHAPTER NINE

A CRACK of fierce laughter shocked Rosa into looking up into Max's dark face.

In a charged moment his arms crushed her against him. He said in a hard-edged, purposeful voice, 'I've wanted you ever since you were sixteen, with legs so long you tripped over them and spectacles you hid behind whenever I looked at you. It was impossible then, and I shouldn't be doing this now, but I've run out of will-power where you're concerned.'

He bent over and lowered her carefully into the hammock.

'Oh—stop!' She jerked upright, clutching the side of the hammock as it swayed. 'What about the man who's searching for bugs—the security man?'

'He won't come out here.'

But she looked furtively around. 'Paparazzi?'

Max smiled at her with glittering eyes and stripped off his shirt. 'We'll be quite safe from stray servants or hopeful paparazzi. Even if our English stalker kayaks in by sea, Security will intercept him before he reaches the beach. No one can see us here; it's perfectly private.'

Afire with desire and anticipation, Rosa watched him drop his shirt onto the honey-coloured stone tiles of the arbour and ease lithely down beside her. He settled his long body a few centimetres from hers.

Although she yearned to reach out and touch him he made no move to come closer, keeping that symbolic distance between them.

In a smoky little whisper she said, 'You make even getting into a hammock a statement of power and grace.'

He surveyed her with hooded, unreadable eyes. 'Is that what you enjoy about me?'

'Of course,' she said, adding with a small, provocative smile, 'amongst other things.' Max's brows lifted. 'What are these other things you like?'

More heat skimmed her cheekbones. 'Well, to start off with—your kindness.'

'Kindness?' His smile twisted into cynicism. 'I'm not kind.'

'Yes, you are,' she told him, longing to stroke the fascinating crease in his cheek, the hard, arrogant line of his jaw, the carved beauty of his mouth. 'You're always very much the boss, but you're unfailingly polite to everyone you deal with—even when you're angry, you don't lose your temper. I've always noticed that; it's actually very intimidating. But it means that although people walk warily around you, they don't have to worry about being shamed.'

His eyes kindled. 'How do you know that?'

'I always knew it.' She smiled a little sadly, remembering the child she'd been, green as grass, at the mercy of her wayward hormones. 'You were kind to me as a kid, and even that summer when I made a nuisance of myself you never tried to humiliate me or embarrass me. Freezing me off so courteously was the best way to deal with it; I was hugely aware of it, but at least it left me some pride. That was kindness.'

'I felt a total heel,' he said ruefully.

'No, a heel would have laughed at me.' She bent forward and kissed the curve of his shoulder, her lips lingering as she felt the muscles tighten and bulge beneath her questing mouth. 'Or encouraged me,' she said soberly.

'I'm not a cad. You were sweet.' The rough undertone to the words sent a rapid ripple of adrenaline through her. 'Such a bright kid, so alert and interested in what was going on, yet so innocent. I enjoyed your forthrightness, your frankness and your blushes. Too much. I was ten years older than you, and there's a hell of a difference between sixteen and twenty-six.'

He bent his head and kissed her, his mouth demanding. Against her lips he said, 'I won't pretend—I can't see that there'll ever be a future for us, Rosa. Even if we could find some way through this maze of lies and cover-ups and ancient rules, I'm too old for you, and with this latest information I'm not a suitable mate anyway.'

Rosa gave a valiant little laugh, because he was just right for her, and the look in his eyes told her he'd never believe that in a million years.

She met his intent gaze without flinching. The future still loomed; this would be all she'd ever have of Max, so she intended to savour every precious, unrepeatable second.

'That's not important. Let's forget about anything else but this.'

He bent to kiss her, but when she sighed and opened her lips to him he lifted his head again. 'This will have to be the only time we can spend together,' he said levelly, meeting her eyes with a warning in his.

Although grief needled through her like pain, she tried to sound mature and sophisticated and definite. 'How long can you stay?'

He paused. 'I haven't told the king yet.'

'Don't go,' she whispered, shattered because when he left her he'd never come back.

'Not yet,' he said ironically, his narrowed gaze pure, molten gold as it searched her face. She thought he was going to put a limit on their stolen days together, but in the end he said, 'As long as I can, Rosa. As long as I dare…'

No promises, no guarantees. Gravely she suggested, 'Then let's not waste a second.'

He said something beneath his breath and kissed her throat, and they lay like that, his mouth against her skin, for blissful moments until she gave a little wriggle against him.

As though he'd forgotten something, he sat

up. Passion, strong and hot and fiercely possessive, still glittered in his eyes, but his voice was
crisp and uncompromising. 'I don't suppose
you're using contraceptive medication?'

'No.' Some of her joy fading, she flushed. Of
course his previous lovers, all sophisticated
beauties, would have seen to that.

He touched her mouth with a long index finger,
his fingertip sending sizzling messages through
her body. 'I'm sorry I was so blunt,' he said, his
eyes gleaming. 'It makes no difference—I'll take
care of you.'

And he got out of the hammock in a swift, lithe
movement and strode out of sight. Dreamily Rosa
basked in the dappled shade of the tree, letting
herself enjoy the sensuous aftermath of his closeness, the urgent hunger for what was to happen.
She pushed away any intrusive thought of caution
or prudence, of the future—of anything but incandescent joy at the prospect of belonging to Max.

Although he made no sound when he came back,
some atavistic instinct warned her of his approach;
she opened her eyes to see him walk around the
corner of the jasmine-laden wall that formed an
almost enclosed courtyard around the jacaranda.

'That didn't take long,' Rosa said huskily. 'Were there any bugs in the villa?'

He smiled at her and lowered himself beside her, and this time there was no space between them. 'He hasn't finished yet, but don't worry, he won't be coming to report.'

Her flash of embarrassment faded under Max's kisses, gentle to begin with and then more demanding until her mouth moulded to his and she kissed him back, her inexperience no match for his potent sexuality. She hoped her love would be enough…

Feverish anticipation swirled through her like some powerful drug, banishing her last reservation, the unwanted voice of caution that warned her this might not be the most sensible thing to be doing.

She simply didn't care. The world could crash around them tomorrow, but she would have today. Daringly she lifted her hands to his head and slid her fingers into his hair, warm silk against her skin.

Against her lips he said with harsh recklessness, 'You have no idea how often I've wanted this—like craving for water in the desert, yet knowing that I'd never find it. Somehow, in spite of everything, you found your way to my life that summer and lodged there like a burr.'

She sighed, her narrowed eyes gleaming. 'I wish I'd known. I used to chastise myself for being so stupid. But when I dreamed I dreamed of you, and no other man has ever made me feel the way a smile from you does.'

'Rosa,' he said with a kind of fierce tenderness, 'that's a hell of a responsibility. No other man?'

Her mouth clung to his for a moment. 'No other man.'

'I hope I can make it good for you.'

Amazed, she lifted her lashes. When she met the crystalline intensity of his gaze she almost quailed. Her dreams had been romantic fantasies; this was Max, the man she loved, earthy and direct, a man who'd intimately known some of the most beautiful women in the world. What did she have to offer him, with her untried body, her un-practised caresses?

'I think that's my line,' she said, her smile lopsided. 'I don't know what I'm doing, but you do.'

'And I find that unbearably stimulating,' he said, lips straightening in self-derision. 'But if you want to call a halt, if you find anything distasteful, tell me.'

Rosa almost laughed. She held his face with her hands, relishing the faint abrasion of his beard against her sensitive palms, and met his eyes with open frankness. 'Nothing you could do would upset me.'

He touched her mouth with his, then kissed her all the way down her throat to the pulse that throbbed in the defenceless hollow there. Rosa stifled a hungry moan when he found the soft lobe of one ear and bit it gently. Sharp delight pierced her from her skin to her innermost being, gathering in a molten pit at the base of her stomach.

She gasped, and he laughed, then kissed the spot underneath her ear before moving on to the sensitive area where her neck met her shoulders. Again he used his teeth to send more of those delicious little darts of pleasure through her.

Sighing, she returned the delicate caress, biting his shoulder before licking the spot with languorous care, inhaling his personal scent and savouring the mixture of salt and musk and compelling masculinity that was Max.

He made an odd sound, halfway between a groan and an exclamation, and turned his head so that his mouth found the pointed, pleading tip of her breast. Ignoring the thin cotton of her bra top, he drew the nipple in.

She'd found his previous caresses enormously exciting and intoxicating, but this was outrageously erotic, each strong movement of his lips sending violently carnal messages to her loins, to every inch of her skin—and to her brain, which promptly gave up any attempt at logic under the sensual overload.

She shuddered with passionate desire, then, terrified that he might think she disliked it, whispered, 'Don't stop.'

He lifted his head and smiled down into her dazzled face, his eyes smouldering in his dark, compelling features.

'I won't,' he assured her, and to prove it flicked open the bikini top, dragging in a sharp breath as he displayed her body, skin glowing and golden against his darker olive tan.

Consumed by a wild compulsion to arch her back and hips against his lean body, Rosa surrendered to it. His arms whipped around her; he was steel clad in velvet, taut and tight-muscled. For several seconds they locked gazes—hers frantic with the need clamouring through her, his hard and blazing.

He said on a harsh note of passion, 'You dazzle me,' and transferred his attention to the other breast.

It was heaven; it was hugely frustrating. She writhed as he summoned a reckless anticipation that built and built under his touch.

Max said gutturally, 'You are utterly beautiful, my sweet one.' He eased her onto her back and kissed the narrow indentation of her waist and her curved hips, his mouth warm and seeking against her sensitised skin.

The hammock swayed, its shifting movements adding another dimension to her heady arousal.

Lips against her flat stomach, he continued, 'You have the eyes and mouth of a houri, with the fresh innocence of youth. You'll never lose that bone-deep frankness. Raised up.'

Obediently she raised her hips, and he showed his experience by ridding her body of its last remaining covering with speed and expertise.

Swamped by a feeling of intense vulnerability at being exposed, Rosa clamped her eyes shut and froze.

There was no humour in his voice when he said softly, 'Lift up your lashes, dearest Rosa. Let me see you.'

Heat burned her skin as she sneaked a look at him. The angular lines of his face were more pronounced, his formidable control barely leashed. She'd expected to see him scrutinising her body with lust, but he was watching her face, and although she sensed the dark, consuming hunger in him, she saw tenderness and understanding there too.

'Don't hide from me,' he said, and kissed the corner of her mouth before swinging off the hammock.

Her eyes widened as he stripped. He was magnificent, she thought, a sudden pulse of desire shaking her free of her virginal fear. By now her eyes were fully accustomed to the shade in the arbour; spell-bound, her gaze slid compulsively over him, registering the elemental beauty of male grace and power and authority.

He would know what to do. She pushed aside the thought of how he'd acquired that knowledge, and swallowed when he donned protection. It didn't seem possible…

But of course it would be. The last qualm vanished in a sensation of complete rightness, of inevitability. Max would make it perfect.

Uncontrollable heat fired every inch of her skin when he turned, and again she didn't dare look when the hammock swayed. Breath locked in her throat, heart thundering in her ears, she waited for his touch.

It came with the sensuous, silken glide of skin over skin as he settled himself against her. 'Sweet Rosa,' he said deeply, easing his arm beneath her. 'Sweet as your name, with a dark, rich bloom that reminds me of the very best Bordeaux…'

Her laugh was fragile. 'Trust you to think of wine.'

He kissed her temple. 'When I look at you I think of rubies and wine and roses, of the subtle perfume of your skin, the quiet richness of your laughter, the dark promise you don't even know lives in your eyes.'

Enchanted, she relaxed, and he kissed her, softly then more fiercely, summoning a desperate need that coiled through her like liquid fire, banishing the last of her inhibitions. She opened her mouth to him, and sighed, and her body arched with involuntary demand.

'So let me see you, my precious one,' he said against her mouth.

Slowly, almost reluctantly, she opened her eyes and looked down the lengths of their bodies, her blush forgotten in the sensual magnificence of Max, her lover. Sunlight through the leaves dappled his flexed body in golden coins, shifting over skin sleek and taut above powerful muscles formed by hard physical work. Hair traced a pattern across his chest then arrowed down towards his—

'Oh, heavens,' she whispered devoutly.

He was so big!

More colour stormed into her cheeks.

He said on a catch of laughter, 'Do you trust me to make sure everything will be all right?'

'I do,' she told him softly. She reached out to trace the line of hair across his torso. His chest lifted and fell as he inhaled, and his skin was hot—so hot that she felt that it might singe her fingertips.

Against his overt power she was slender and

pale; always tall, she'd never felt so fragile and womanly in her life.

Or so safe.

She looked into eyes almost closed, so that only shards of molten gold showed through his long, black lashes. Bravely, fingertips tingling, she followed the arrow of hair down.

But before she reached his waist he stopped her. 'Better not,' he said in a low, raw voice. 'I'm already too close to the edge. Later you can do whatever you want to.'

Intoxicated by the thought that she had such power over him, she left that exploration for another time, raising her hand to stroke a finger down the crease in his cheek, loving him with her eyes and touch.

'If it does hurt,' she said in a smoky voice, 'it will be worth it. Don't worry—I spent a lot of time riding my horse when I was a kid, and at school they said that helped.'

He laughed quietly, and turned his head to catch her fingertip in his teeth, closing them just enough to send a series of tantalising pleasure-pain reflexes through her. Stoking them, he eased his fingers between her legs, creating a wave of such intense response that she bucked and set the hammock swaying crazily.

Somehow, she realised dazedly, he used the motion of the hammock to increase the acute, feverish hunger she felt when he touched her so intimately. Her flesh tightened around him and he said something she didn't hear as swift, unasked-for rapture took her by surprise and she groaned and convulsed around his fingers.

'Ah, Rosa,' he said when it was over. 'You surprise me constantly.'

She lifted heavy eyelids. 'What do we do now?'

His lips moved in a keen, almost savage smile that drove her heart-rate even higher. 'We do it—properly.'

The hammock lurched slightly as he positioned himself over her. Desperately she gripped his hips, fingers gripping his sweat-damp skin, and before she had time to think he pushed into her.

There was resistance, and yes, a little pain.

Eyes widening, she gasped, 'It's all right—*oh*!' as he thrust home to lodge himself in her. She felt invaded, stretched and yet—whole for the first time in her life.

The incendiary thrill he'd produced with his

clever fingers began to sizzle again, deep inside. Heart drumming madly, she looked up into a face made brutal by primal need, and her body tensed in eager anticipation.

'M-Max,' she stammered, unable to think, unable to do anything but react when he began to move once more.

'I'm not hurting you?' he asked in a raw voice.

The gentle rocking of the hammock sent skin licking against skin in sensuous communion.

'Oh, no. It's—wonderful,' she breathed.

He dropped a kiss on her mouth, holding it captive as he started to pull back.

Chilled, she cried urgently, 'No!' and pressed her thighs together to stop him leaving her.

'It's all right,' he promised, setting up a rhythm that marched with the wildfire thunder of her blood and the honeyed fire that his slow, deliberate advance and retreat caused.

Rosa groaned, unable to do anything but lift her hips and arch her back in an unspoken plea. He smiled—another tight, tigerish smile—but held her to the rhythm until waves of sensation rose again, but stronger and more intense than before, spreading and building through her body.

She called out something—she didn't know what—as one last surge carried her into another dimension where the only limits were how much delicious sensation her body could cope with and still survive. Every muscle strung taut as a bow, every cell alive and aware, every nerve stretched to its utmost capacity, she crested and soared into mindless ecstasy.

'Rosa!'

Still lost in fulfilment, she forced up her lashes. Above her, Max's face was stripped of everything but untamed need as he thrust one last time before the rapture overwhelmed him too. Head flung back, body straining, he drove deep into her, and she thought with aching poignancy that she'd never forget this.

Never...

Dismissing the future, she concentrated on recalling everything, from the soft sibilance of the waves on the shore to the perfume of the jasmine, the heat of his body, relaxed and heavy on her, the strength he'd held in check for her...

She would carve this memory in her brain, know it so well that she'd never forget.

Max turned onto his side and hugged her to

him. 'I'm glad you rode that horse so much,' he said solemnly.

She giggled, then yawned. Shocked, she realised that she wanted nothing more than to go to sleep.

'Sleep now; I won't go away,' he said, and watched with narrowed eyes as exhaustion dragged her down into the most wonderful sleep she'd ever experienced.

When she woke he was still watching her, his expression so remote and controlled that she flinched and muttered, 'What time is it?'

'Who cares?'

She gave a tart smile. 'I do, because any minute now the servants will be back to prepare dinner.'

'It's a poor life that's ruled by servants,' he said with irony.

Laughing, she scrambled out, standing for a few precious seconds to gloat over him, big and powerful and hers—for the moment—sprawled in the aftermath of sated passion.

'Like what you see?' he asked, his smile a definite challenge.

He was aroused. After a startled, blushing

glance, Rosa turned away to collect her scattered clothes. 'Very much,' she said sedately.

She had started to pull on undergarments when he came up and turned her into his arms, and kissed her, swift and hard and passionately.

But when she clung he set her away, reminding her with a twisted smile, 'Servants.'

Together they went into the cool dimness of the villa, where she said awkwardly, 'Where do you want to sleep?'

'With you,' he said, amusement and desire gleaming in his eyes. 'But I'm not going to. See how servants make life difficult?'

'They wouldn't gossip—'

She checked her impulsive words. They'd made love—at her insistence—but that didn't mean he'd want to sleep with her. Fighting back an obscure hurt, she said coolly, 'Actually, you're right. No sense in tempting fate, is there? I'll put you along the hall.'

Of course his room wasn't made up, and she discovered with some dismay that there were no towels in his bathroom. 'I don't even know where they're kept,' she said, feeling stupid.

He looked down at her, his eyes heavy-lidded

and amused. 'Then I'll use yours, if I may. And we can shower together.'

Her bones melted. Was there any more wonderful word than *together*? Trying very hard to sound sophisticated, she said, 'I'd like that.'

Stomach fluttering, she led him to her big, airy room, with the sea glinting between the blades of the shutters, half closed against the late afternoon sun. She hoped that they'd make love again in the shower, but, although he soaped her with slow, caressing strokes and was clearly aroused, he didn't suggest it.

Newly emboldened, Rosa did.

'I'd like to very much,' he said, eyes glinting as he traced a heart in the soap bubbles on one breast, 'but although you might not be sore now, you're likely to be if we do it again. Wait until tomorrow morning.'

And although she pulled a face, she agreed. His consideration charmed her. But then, she thought, when he'd left to change, now that she'd made love with Max everything seemed richer, more exciting, almost as though their union had embroidered her life with extra meaning.

After dinner, when stars were pricking the

midnight-blue sky and the servants had left again, she looked across the table on the terrace and murmured, 'I hope you're not going to be noble for too long.'

He was leaning back in his chair, one long-fingered hand curved around the stem of his half-empty wineglass, the light of the candles flickering on his handsome face. He seemed lost in thought, but when she spoke he looked up and laughed.

'No,' he said. 'Anyway, there are other ways to pleasure you.'

And that hidden thrill of excitement ran through her like wildfire.

'Let's go to bed,' he said in a different voice.

CHAPTER TEN

AFTER dinner Max showed her some of the ways he could pleasure her without inducing soreness.

They induced exhaustion, though—an ecstatic, sated weariness that saw Rosa lying limply in his arms as she asked in a drained voice, 'Do you mind if I stay like this for the night?'

'I'd enjoy it very much—too much!—but we need to establish that we're sleeping in different rooms,' he said reluctantly.

More confident now of his desire, she pouted. 'No one would know. Your security man said the house was free from bugs, and we could rumple your bed.'

'There are other ways of finding things out—telephoto lenses, for example.'

Gently but deliberately, he eased her off, and got out of the bed without turning on the light. The moon had risen, tiger-striping him with silver bars through the shutters. He looked big and powerful and alien, even though she now knew every smooth, strong bulge of muscle, every clean line of sinew and bone, the way he smelled, his taste…

Chilled, Rosa lifted herself on one elbow and watched him dress. 'Here?'

'It's possible,' he said casually. 'Not likely, I agree, but we have to be circumspect. Anyway, you need a good night's sleep.'

She flushed. 'I think I'd probably sleep better if you were with me,' she said thoughtfully.

A distinctly predatory smile sent hot shivers down her spine. 'I doubt if you'd sleep much at all,' he countered.

Laughing and pink, she acknowledged the probable truth of that.

He sobered. 'So sleep well, my treasure.'

But once he'd gone, her tiredness left her. Outside the sea hushed onto the beach, and crickets sang in the olive trees on the rocky headland.

Sick at heart, she forced herself to face the future. There was no one else in line for the succession; by default the throne would come to her.

Panic kicked beneath her ribs. How could she govern with any degree of authority or wisdom?

She knew little of political science, even less of economics and nothing of constitutional policy—her career path couldn't have been better chosen to deprive her of the right sort of skills.

Even when most other countries elected to become republics, the islanders had clung to the monarchy. Things had moved slowly over the years because the king was deeply conservative, and most of his subjects seemed content with the status quo.

A woman ruler would be viewed with huge suspicion.

Yet what would be the alternative? The sort of civil war that had almost wrecked Niroli only a generation ago?

Hours later she was still awake, eyes hot and aching as she mulled over impossible schemes to secure some sort of future for her and Max. Goaded by restlessness, she scrambled out of bed and walked barefoot across to the doors that opened onto a balcony. Her nightdress floating around her, she paced across to the balustrade, searching for some ease of mind in the calm serenity of the familiar view.

Tiles still warm from the heat of the day were smooth beneath her bare feet. No wind ruffled the black and silver garden or the olive groves on the headland. The crickets had finally given up their shrill calls; no nightingale sang in the trees, no tiny brown frogs croaked. The only sound was the soft hush of the sea on the shore.

Mind buzzing, she tried to work out how she was going to deal with any summons from the king, but her wayward brain kept returning to the fact that Max didn't love her, and she loved him. Skin heating, she recalled the moments when she must have made that pretty obvious.

Oh, he'd been everything any woman would ever want in her first lover, she thought sadly—gentle, considerate, sexy as hell, tender and fierce by turns...

He'd taken her to heaven and somewhere much more earthy in his arms, then brought her back down without treating her like a novice.

A reminiscent little shiver tightened her skin. He'd made her feel cherished, she thought, and a silent sob ached in her throat. His experience hadn't intimidated her; he'd used it to convince her that she was every bit as desirable as any of the women he'd known previously, every bit as worth taking to bed.

She would always love him for that.

Now, listening to the sound of silence, she tried to be grateful that he hadn't told her the easy lie.

He could have said it. 'I love you.'

Three small words people said in the heat of desire. She had friends who'd been told that, only to discover that what their lovers had meant was, 'I want you.'

They'd expected her friends to understand it was a lie, the thing a man said to a woman in the heat of passion or when she wanted reassurance.

But Max had too much integrity to pretend a love he didn't feel.

The ache in her heart turned into an emptiness that would echo through all the years ahead.

Instinct warned her that once she'd donned the massive crown of Niroli, heavy with gold and pearls and ancient diamonds, she'd never see Max again.

He was worthy of those symbols, a leader strong enough to wear the crown, to carry the sceptre with its relic of the first ruling king, a huge ruby that had decorated the hilt of the sword he'd wielded when he'd turned an island of robber counts and bandits into a nation.

Rosa knew she wasn't worthy. She'd be nothing more than a hollow person, a decorated doll trotted out to appease the islanders, always conscious that she was very much a substitute.

Max's voice, pitched to reach only her from the next balcony, made her jump. 'What is it, Rosa?'

'I won't be able to do it,' she said desperately, her mind darting this way and that. Her hands clenched on the balustrade, and without looking across she blurted, 'Max, I don't know how to rule a village, let alone a country.'

Silence stretched between them, taut with tension and unspoken words as she gripped the stone until her knuckles whitened.

Still in that quiet voice, he said, 'Go back into your room. Don't switch on your light.'

Head buzzing, she walked inside. The door into the passage opened and Max came noiselessly in. The moon through the shutters gave enough light for her to see that he was still dressed.

Before he could say anything she said, 'I'm sorry. You have enough to think about without hearing me whine. Go back to bed.'

'The prospect of ruling Niroli is not an easy one for any of us.' He came across and slid his arm around her shoulders, hugging her to him.

Gratefully she leaned against him, taking courage from his strength. 'The whole business must be hell for you!'

'Difficult,' he admitted. 'And, yes, I know it's going to be more than difficult for my mother and the king, even if we manage to keep it quiet. But it won't be hell. I never wanted to rule.'

She shuddered. 'Neither do I. Max, I'm so scared. I haven't the training in business you have, I don't know how to organise anything bigger than a lab.'

Alarmed by a dangerous wobble in her voice, she folded her lips, clamping down tightly on the rest of her fears.

He said quietly, 'That's exactly how I felt when I realised I was next in line.'

'But you've had executive experience,' she wailed. 'I haven't. And you're a leader—you always were. I wasn't even a monitor at school!'

'Hush,' he said, smoothing back the tumbled mass of hair from her brow. 'You're clever, you're popular with the people and you'll learn.' His voice altered and he pulled her around into his arms properly, holding her so that she could feel his very obvious erection. 'You're too tense,' he said, his voice thickening subtly. 'I think I can give you something else to think about.'

She gave a voluptuous little wiggle, delighting in his instant response. 'Are you manipulating me with sex?' she asked daringly.

His smile was white and definitely buccaneering. 'I suspect I am. Do you mind?'

'Not at all,' she said demurely.

He picked her up and dropped her onto the bed. 'No, don't take off your nightgown,' he said, when she sat up to do just that.

She wondered why, but he was shedding his clothes and she was happy to watch him. He came down beside her and held her against him.

'Why do you want me to stay clothed?' she asked, caught by an odd unease.

'Because I don't trust myself,' he said, and banished her next question with his kisses.

When she was pliant and sighing in his arms,

he slid the ribbon straps down over her shoulders, baring her breasts, and began kissing them, taking his time.

It was heaven; Rosa pushed from her mind the fact that he must have made love to a lot of women to be so knowledgeable about how female bodies responded.

In a very short time she no longer cared.

Max made love to her with utter absorption, his mouth and hands skilled and tormenting, gentle when she needed gentleness, then fierce, until her hips were twisting on the bed, her breath coming in short, sharp pants between her famished lips.

He wouldn't let her touch him. 'No, this is for you.'

Wild sensations rioting through her, she learned what it was like to be worshipped with lips and hands and intense, savage words, to be kissed all over, to be caressed until she moaned with delicious frustration.

And then, at last, when she could bear it no longer, to be brought to instant satisfaction with his mouth.

Shuddering in the shattering aftermath, she

clutched his sweat-slicked body and said hoarsely, 'But you—what about you?'

He hugged her. 'It's all right.'

'No,' she said with feverish intensity, 'it's not all right. It was wonderful, but I need to—I want to do something for you.'

He was silent for so long she wondered if she'd said something totally outrageous. Uncertainly, she looked up at him, her gaze picking out the honed contours of his face, and her heart over-flowed with passionate regret. She intended to take everything she could from these precious days, because the memories were going to have to last a lifetime.

'Please,' she whispered, and kissed one dark, flat nipple, incredulous when she felt it stir beneath her tongue.

It seemed that what she liked applied to him too.

Eyes gleaming, he lifted her face and scru-tinised it. 'Then I am at your command,' he said, an undernote of raw hunger sending more thrills through her.

He rolled over onto his back, and spread out his arms. A little nervously, Rosa began to touch him, her hands fluttering across smooth sleek skin, tracing firm muscles, the hollows and curves of his body.

And where her hands went, her mouth followed; in the most elemental way of all she explored him, kissing, licking, noting with keen satisfaction when he became very taut and still, his hands clenching at his sides. In the end, a groan was torn from his throat.

'Sadist,' he ground out.

Laughing, she kissed his mouth, and stretched herself out along him. His body jerked beneath her; with a muttered curse he pushed her off and got off the bed.

'Protection,' he stated in a driven voice before she had time to react to the brutal rejection.

No! Despair and defiance surged darkly through her. A baby of Max's… But it was impossible.

Nevertheless, every cell in her body thrilled to the thought, even as she watched him search for the small packet.

When he came back to the bed he said, 'Are you sore?'

Rosa wanted to say, 'You can't hurt me,' but she knew she was wrong. Honestly she said, 'Probably, but I don't care.'

He lay down beside her and pulled her on top of him. 'You can regulate the process better this way.'

'The *process*?' she spluttered and laughed and he laughed too, and with laughter and passion and infinite care, she guided him into her.

He was right. She could control their love-making, and it had a whole new feel to it, voluptuously different yet just as exciting as it had been the first time. When at last they reached the peak she cried out, and collapsed onto him in rapturous release.

He held her there, his chest rising and falling as he dragged air into his lungs, his big body shuddering, his arms wonderfully secure around her.

Sated, secure as she'd never been before, Rosa went to sleep in his arms, but she woke the next morning once more alone in the big bed. Stretching a body that ached pleasantly in all sorts of new and interesting ways, she smiled into her pillow and sat up.

Whatever the future had in store for them, she'd make the most of the time they had. She'd banish every fear and worry from her mind, and concentrate on enjoying this time with Max.

'What would you like to do today?' Max asked

over breakfast, eaten beneath the feathery
canopy of a silk tree in the courtyard.

'What I did yesterday,' she said coolly,
blushing when he smiled at her.

'I think we can manage that, but we should go
out to dinner soon.'

She sent him a mischievous glance, meeting
the burnished green-gold sheen of his gaze with
a smile. 'Why?'

'If we wait until later it might be too obvious
that we're not just cousins who decided to
holiday at the same time,' he said drily. 'And
there are definitely paparazzi about.'

'In that case,' she conceded easily, 'perhaps
we'd better go tonight.'

Any obvious signs of their new relationship
wouldn't come from him, she thought as she got
ready that evening. It was impossible to read
what he was thinking or feeling behind the magnificent mask of his features.

She'd have to rein in the blushes that still
heated her skin when he surveyed her in a certain
way; she'd be reserved and a little distant. Which
meant cosmetics. After making up carefully—
refined but not overtly sexy, Kate would have

called the look—she got into the black dress with its saucy white polka dots, left her hair loose and casual, and slipped on the only pair of sandals she'd brought with her.

They chose a small restaurant in the biggest town on the island, and were greeted with pleasure by the proprietor, although he immediately said, 'A table inside, Highness? There is a photographer around.'

Max asked, 'How long has he been here?'

'Three or four days.' The proprietor shrugged and spread his hands. 'He is not with the journalist as far as we can tell, but both are asking too many questions. It is because of the succession,' he said, nodding sagely as he looked at Max.

Some unspoken message passed between them. Aloud, Max said, 'Then we'll eat inside, thank you.'

'We do not gossip about our family,' the restaurant owner said energetically, snapping his fingers at the waiter. 'You will permit me to offer you wine from my brother's vineyard? You enjoyed the nineteen ninety-five last time you dined here; this is the nineteen ninety-nine vintage.'

Max said, 'My cousin and I would be honoured. A magnificent year.'

The proprietor snapped his fingers again, and the waiter approached with the bottle. As he opened it with a flourish the owner resumed, 'We are waiting for you to come back to the island and do for us what you have done for the wine-makers of Niroli.'

Max tasted it, then raised his glass in salute. 'You don't need me,' he said calmly. 'This is superb.'

The owner smiled and bowed. 'Thank you, Your Highness. I'll tell my brother that you approve. Because of your success on Niroli he has worked hard to improve both his grape-growing and his wine-making methods.'

Clearly, Max was hugely popular. Taking a tiny sip of her wine, Rosa thought bleakly that he deserved the throne.

Last night, in spite of her resolution to ignore the problem of the succession, she'd lain listening to his breathing and tried to work out some escape from the tangle they were in.

It was hopeless. For them to be together without scandal and a constitutional crisis, their total lack of relationship needed to be established, and there was no way of doing that without proclaiming Queen Eva's infidelity to the world.

Yet the king would never let that happen; his pride wouldn't allow it. And although she ached to walk away from the whole legacy of inheritance and tradition, in her heart she understood the old man who'd fought a savage civil war to hold his country together. He came from a different age; to him, the only thing that mattered would be that his family continued to rule Niroli, no matter how badly.

Heart swelling, she glanced at Max. It took all her will-power to look at him with nothing more than the pleasant affection one would give a cousin.

He said, 'What would you like to eat?'

Transferring her smile to the owner, she said perceptively, 'You know what I like.'

'Fettucini with pesto and pine nuts,' he returned immediately, beaming. 'Even when you were a child on your mother's knee you wanted my fettucini.'

'It means home to me,' she told him. 'My mother's cook couldn't make it like you.'

'Ah, because the secret ingredient is love. And although love might be hard to reveal, it is always noticed.' He bowed and left them.

'I wonder what he meant by that,' she said uneasily.

Max shrugged, his eyes hooded. 'Nothing. Or a veiled warning. Whatever it was, we don't have to worry about Vincenzo talking. He's discreet and insular, as are most of the islanders.'

Quelling an urge to look around, she said, 'Do you really think—'

'Relax. No paparazzo will come in here.'

In spite of the magnificent food, Rosa's tension increased as the evening wore on. She was relieved when at last it wound down with compliments to the chef and the proprietor, farewells and smiles. The car was drawn up outside, but as they left the restaurant a flash popped several times.

After one direct glance at the photographer, Max ushered Rosa into the front passenger seat before getting behind the wheel.

Once in, she shivered, and leaned her head back against the seat and closed her eyes, pretending to be tired. Max's anger, a dark force, pulsed in the car as he set it in motion.

Back at the villa she stopped at the foot of the stairs and said, 'How long has the press been snooping on the island?'

He paused, then said deliberately, 'Since Giovanni and I sent samples to be tested.'

Rosa froze, scanning his shuttered face. 'Do you think there's a connection?'

'There shouldn't be,' he said, his voice dispassionate.

'But you suspect there might be.'

He shrugged. 'I don't know. But someone at the clinic could have a contact with the media. It doesn't seem likely, because they'd already know the truth, but it is a possibility.'

Her mind working frantically, she said, 'Is that why you came here?'

'Partly,' he admitted after a pause. He examined her pale face with hooded eyes. 'I wanted to make sure that the villa was checked for bugs and that security was up to scratch, but the sensible thing would have been to stay away. As that wasn't an option, we have to behave as normally as possible.'

For once—because he wanted to be with her—he'd let his heart rule his head. Dowsing the swift flare of elation that realisation caused, she said slowly, 'Why would paparazzi sniff around the royal island? The people here are notorious for their loyalty to the family.'

'This is where Giovanni and Queen Eva conducted their illicit affair,' Max told her, each word dropping like a stone.

The cold patch beneath her ribs expanded. 'I see. But surely—you said yourself that the islanders don't talk.'

He didn't try to appease her with platitudes. 'Anything's possible. I always assume the best and prepare for the worst.' Metallic, opaque eyes met hers. 'Today my head of security warned me that a man who appears to be an ordinary tourist is trying to find out about that long-ago love affair.'

When she gasped, he went on sardonically, 'Nothing so crass as straight questions. Conversations have been struck up with old people who'd have been around then, directed along certain paths, innuendoes made. So far with no success that I'm aware of, but it's possible that there was gossip then, and that someone will spill the beans.'

She nodded, feeling sick. 'I suppose that's why I've been feeling as though someone's watching me—that strange sensation between the shoulder blades. Max, it was dangerous to come here.'

'Don't worry,' he said instantly. 'You'll be well protected if the news breaks. I can get you out of here within twenty minutes of any trouble, and within an hour you'll be leaving Niroli for New Zealand.'

'I'm not worried about myself.' She should be as staunch as he was, not weakly begging to be reassured.

He gave her a savage pirate's smile, eyes glinting with something too close to recklessness for her liking. It faded, replaced by his usual un-compromising control. 'I don't care what they might say about me, but there are others—my mother, the king—who have to be considered.' He frowned, and took her hand, urging her up the stairs. 'Has all this spoiled the evening?'

'The evening was great,' she said.

It would have been even better if they hadn't had to pretend they were nothing more to each other than cousins who happened to be spending a holiday in the same place, but she wasn't going to whine.

'It's been—wonderful,' she said at the top of the stairs. 'I'll never forget it.'

'It's not over yet. Come here.'

But when she moved into his arms she wouldn't look at him until he tipped her chin with a lean brown finger. Eyes glinting gold, he said, 'Shall I show you what I wanted to do for the whole evening?'

Her slow smile of promise sent his hormones crazy. 'I'd love that,' she told him huskily.

But later, when he'd thoroughly and expertly made love to her, she thought that the evening had been tarnished. Like all lovers, she wanted to be open and frank about her love; now she knew it could never happen.

Max said into the darkness, 'What's the matter?'

'Oh, I'm just railing at fate,' she said on a note of irony.

'Railing never achieved anything.' He took her in his arms and held her against his heart, and she went to sleep with its slow, steady, completely reliable rhythm in her ears.

In fact she slept so deeply that when she woke

alone in her bed early in the morning she felt as though she'd been heavily sedated.

After her shower she wandered out onto the balcony, to comb her wet hair. The sun had long been up, and the sea glittered as the waves frisked into the bay.

Over breakfast she asked tentatively, 'Are you sure you'll leave Niroli?' She could bear being Queen if he stayed. 'It's your home…' Her voice trailed away.

His face set into formidable lines of authority. 'I'll leave. Even if the king allowed it—and he won't—staying will be impossible.'

Dismayed, she objected, 'But you love the place! It's wouldn't be fair to drive you away—'

'Nothing is fair about this situation.' Cold cynicism hardened his voice and his face was un-readable.

Visualising the torment she'd go through if he stayed, and she was eventually forced to take the throne, she shivered. Inevitably she'd give herself away. 'I suppose it wouldn't work.'

'It would not,' he said with uncompromising decision.

She forced herself to sound practical. 'So if

it happens, where would you go? I know you have an apartment in London and another in New York—would you live in one of those?'

'I might go to New Zealand,' he said, and smiled sardonically at the surprise she couldn't hide. 'I've spent the past years dragging an ancient industry into the twenty-first century; I'd like to produce new wines in a largely untried *terroir.*'

Rosa sprang to the defence of the place she'd learned to love. 'They do brilliant white wines.'

'I know, and all credit to them. They've even produced some superb reds. If I were setting up there, I'd try grapes from Niroli in the north where it's warmer, and pinot noir in the south, against the mountains.'

'In other words,' she said, entering into the spirit of this, 'you don't plan to be content with a vineyard, you want to develop an industry. Once an entrepreneur, always an entrepreneur!'

They spent the rest of the meal discussing the possibilities—pretending, she realised, that one day they'd be able to do it together.

But at the end of the meal she said quietly, 'Can you stop the sale of your business affairs, or is it too late?'

'Yes; I've already put that on hold.'

'Won't it cause the sort of gossip you don't want?'

'No. The whole thing's been very discreetly handled so far—kept in the family, so to speak.' He gave a mirthless smile. 'No one's going to worry about a hiatus.'

That morning they went to visit her parents' grave. The king had wanted his son buried in the vault in the cathedral in the capital, but Rosa and her siblings had fought for the island, which her parents had loved and where they'd spent their happiest times. The tiny church in the nearest village had offered a sanctuary in hallowed ground, and eventually the king had given in.

The villagers stayed respectfully away while Rosa laid flowers she'd picked on the hillsides around the villa on the grave where they'd been buried together.

Tears pricked her eyes, but as she stood there and looked out over the sea they both loved so much, she said quietly, 'I think they're at peace. They had problems—' briefly her mind skated to Adam Ryder, the product of her father's one indiscretion '—but they loved each other.'

The next few days were spent in heated, erotic seclusion. The sex, as Rosa had always known it would be, was wonderful—a true communion of bodies and spirit—but in the years to come it would be the talking she'd miss.

Not that they agreed on everything; in some ways they couldn't have been more different, although arguing with him was as much fun as agreeing, and she had never felt so exhilarated, so stimulated as when they clashed.

And they talked about Niroli's future; very soon Rosa realised that Max was grooming her for the position of ruler.

When she taxed him with it he smiled wryly. 'If the worst comes to the worst, I won't have to worry that I left you completely unprepared.' He paused, then said evenly, 'I won't be able to mentor you if you are forced onto the throne. There must be no hint of scandal—for some years you'll be watched exceedingly carefully, and not just by the paparazzi. The islanders will be wary. And although I will give you my complete support, we mustn't contact each other at all.'

'There's always email,' she said, despising herself.

He looked straight at her, his brows together. 'Even email can be breached,' he said quietly. 'No. A clean break, Rosa. It's the only way.'

CHAPTER ELEVEN

ROSA closed her eyes, her whole being rebelling at Max's brutal decision. She wanted to wail, to weep and scream and throw herself onto the ground, sobbing and beating her fists in an orgy of grief.

Of course she did none of that. Training held, she thought, scanning his beloved face with painful intensity. She'd been trained to be a princess; now it seemed she might have to undergo further, more stringent instruction.

'It's too dangerous,' Max stated. 'Rosa, you'll make an excellent ruler for Niroli. You're clever—you learn fast. You have excellent people skills. You're prepared to compromise without losing your integrity.'

Her lips trembled. 'Thank you. If—if it comes to that, I so hope you're right.'

At least after the last few days of intense discussion, she had a much better idea of how Niroli worked. She still dreaded the thought of having to take up a position she wasn't qualified for, but Max's confidence in her ability to cope had heartened her.

She'd always cherish the knowledge of his belief in her.

Towards the end of their stolen days together, Rosa and he attended a formal blessing of the fishing fleet, then left the villagers to enjoy themselves at the fiesta that followed, giving the servants the two days off.

After that she'd leave the island, and they'd probably never see each other alone again.

They spent the time together in erotic laziness, worshipping at the shrine of their passion, and each hour she fell further and further in love with Max.

Once he said lazily, but with enough emphasis to make her lift her head from his chest, 'We're masochists. This is only going to make things harder when we're no longer together.'

Yawning, Rosa settled her hips even more firmly against his. He stirred, and she chuckled, a low, intimate little sound. 'I know, but I'm so glad you came.' Her voice deepened into intensity. 'If this is all I'm going to have, then it will be worth it.'

He smiled and kissed her shoulder. 'I told myself to stay away.'

'Did you?' She slid a wicked tongue into his ear, enjoying the sudden hardening of his body beneath her. 'That inconvenient conscience of yours, I suppose. How does it feel now?'

'Sated, like the rest of me.' But he turned her over onto her back and stroked her from her high breasts to the juncture of her legs, his hand lingering with potent carnal effect on her satin skin.

'Mmm, me too,' she said huskily, finding him with unerring accuracy.

But his head came up abruptly and his eyes narrowed as he looked across to the window, shuttered against the afternoon sun.

Rosa froze. Eyes dilating, she opened her mouth to ask what he'd heard.

He dipped his head and breathed against her ear, 'Get dressed,' and then left her alone and exposed in the big bed, pacing with noiseless steps across the tiles to stop just inside the open doors onto the balcony.

The closed shutters protected him from prying eyes. Shuttered gold barred his lean body, poised and lethally powerful as any predator. Moving as silently as she could, Rosa pulled on shorts and a T-shirt, combed her hair and was coming across to stand beside him when he gestured.

She stopped, separating out the music of the waves, the sleepy call of a dove. From somewhere below came a gentle scraping noise—the sort of sound someone might make if they were trying to climb the vine that wound its way up the wall of the villa.

An intruder? Unconsciously she gnawed her lip, watching Max with wide, frightened eyes.

He turned and took her hand, pulling her well away from the windows. In a voice that was perfectly clear yet pitched for her ears only, he said, 'Go into the bathroom. You've had your siesta, and now you're washing your face and getting dressed. If he gets onto the balcony, yell for me and run out into the hall.'

Nerves twanging, she tiptoed into the bathroom, ran taps, cleaned her teeth, washed her face and dried it, then put on make-up carefully, hoping it hid the traces of the long hours spent in Max's arms.

Adrenaline boosted her confidence, so that she felt she could take on the world and win. Nevertheless, she had to stop and take a deep breath when she could no longer put off going out into the bedroom.

It was a huge let-down—and an almighty relief—when her stabbing gaze found no one in sight—not in the room, not silhouetted against the shutters from outside. Heart pounding, she walked across to the shutters and flung them back.

Again, nobody, but from somewhere—in the garden, she was almost certain—she heard voices. She hesitated. Should she go out? Yes. Clearly Max had wanted everything to seem entirely normal, and if she'd just woken from her siesta she'd definitely be curious and want to see what was happening.

So she ignored the hollowness in her stomach and stepped out onto the balcony. Beneath the silk tree two men were facing each other—one a total stranger, now firmly held in Max's grip.

Outraged and a little frightened, Rosa snatched

up her mobile phone and ran down the stairs and out into the brazen heat.

Intent on each other, neither man noticed her arrival. She relaxed when she realised that, although their attitudes proclaimed antagonism, they were talking rather than squaring up at each other. In fact, when she stopped in the deep shade of a carob tree Max let the intruder go.

'Get the hell out of here,' he said contemptuously in English. 'If I see you again on this island I'll call the police.'

The intruder flicked an insolent glance at Rosa. 'Why aren't you calling them now?' he asked.

Max gave him a look that should have shut him up. 'On your way,' he commanded.

The other man asked, 'How would it affect your chances of being King if your grandfather discovered that you're sleeping with your cousin?'

Rosa's jaw dropped. The sheer vulgarity of his words shocked her. Horrified, she watched as Max took a swing at the man, knocking him to the ground. 'Try that,' he said between his teeth as the man scrambled to his feet, 'and I'll bring both you and your rag of a newspaper to bankruptcy.'

'You can't prove you're not,' the man shot back, keeping well out of Max's reach as he nursed his jaw.

In a tone that lifted the hairs on Rosa's skin, Max said, 'Are you trying to blackmail me?'

'Just checking.' The journalist took a hasty step backwards. 'OK, I'll believe that you're keeping to your own beds. But what would the king say if he knew that at about the time your father was conceived his wife was having a hot and heavy affair with the keeper of the royal vineyards? That might explain why your father showed no signs of the Fierezza charm and looks.'

Horrified, Rosa watched Max's fists clench at his sides.

Contemptuously he said, 'I won't honour that with an answer. You have an hour to get off the island. Don't bother trying to get back onto it. Your employer will be hearing from me.'

The reporter shrugged. 'Ever heard of DNA testing?'

Max merely lifted a scornful brow. 'You're using up your time.'

The intruder sent another glance at Rosa. 'Your

cousin's a scientist—she'll know all about it. Get her to fill you in on how easy it is to collect samples. All it takes is a maid with a grudge.'

Max said lethally, 'Rosa, ring the police.'

'Hey—you can't do that.'

'Watch me,' Max said with cold menace as Rosa tapped in the number that took her straight to the local police station.

'I've got proof,' the man shouted. 'Photographic proof.'

It took every bit of Rosa's self-control not to let her gaze fly to Max's face. Sick apprehension built inside her and she silently urged the police to answer.

Max's icy voice cut through the hot silence of the afternoon. 'You're lying.'

'I'm not! It's impossible to keep an affair secret in a place like this and Queen Eva's made enemies here—not everyone thinks the sun rises and sets because the royal family tells it to.' The journalist's words tumbled over each other in his urgency to get them out. 'I shot a snap of Giovanni What's-his-name, and sent it to an expert in forensic medicine. He checked it against you and your brother and he says that it's a ninety per cent chance that you're all descended from the grape-grower, not the king.'

Before Rosa could process this, a voice spoke in her ear. She wrenched her thoughts together enough to tell the flustered clerk at the police station briefly what was happening, and was assured that someone would be at the villa in ten minutes.

Max said nothing, his silence made more ominous by the unreadable mask of his face.

'Hey, listen,' the reporter protested, uneasy now. His eyes darted from Max's cold, intimidating face to Rosa's. Presumably judging her to be the easiest to sway, he said, 'Princess, tell him that he can't come over all feudal—those days are past.'

'You're trespassing,' she said, hoping her contempt hid her fear. 'It's illegal here. Besides, I heard you trying to blackmail him.'

'I didn't,' he yelped. 'Listen, he knows all about it. Ask him why he and the old man had DNA testing before he came here. Go on, ask him!'

'You disgust me,' she retorted.

'He knows he's not a Fierezza.' He grinned.

'Anyway, it doesn't matter. The results are with my office in London.'

Rosa hoped that her shock didn't appear in her expression. She didn't dare look at Max.

The journalist said eagerly, 'He's keeping you out of your rightful place as Queen of Niroli, and he's trying to hang on to power by making you fall in love with him.'

'Have you ever thought of writing fiction?' she said frigidly, not daring to look at Max.

Touching the jaw where Max had hit him, the journalist blustered, 'You assaulted me—or isn't it illegal in Niroli for fake princes to punch out the press? You can't put me in prison. I've got a right to tell the truth.'

'I doubt if you'd recognise truth if it approached you in a bikini. It is illegal to attempt blackmail and to trespass,' Max said with lethal scorn. 'However, what happens to you will be decided by our courts.' He looked up as the sound of an engine drowned out the soft whisper of the waves. 'Ah, here are the police.'

The journalist made a sudden dash for the beach. He took only two steps before Max brought him down, sending his small camera flying.

'You bastard!' the journalist howled, scrabbling for his equipment.

Ignoring his shouted imprecations, Max dragged him to his feet and twisted his arm up his back.

Rosa breathed a heartfelt sigh when two policemen ran down the path and took over.

One hauled the reporter out of sight, while the other spoke respectfully to Max. Then he too left.

Grimly Max said, 'That should keep him out of mischief for a couple of days, but we're not going to be able to silence him. If he's telling the truth—and I suspect he is—his tabloid is going to spill the beans in what I imagine is their biggest story of the century so far. I have to tell the king, and you must leave Niroli today.'

Pain clawed Rosa, but she fought it back. She couldn't break now. Later—when no one could see her—she might be able to accept that once more he'd put his duty before her. She had to accept it. 'When—when will I see you next?'

'I don't know.' He wasn't looking at her. 'Possibly never.'

It was the answer she expected. Wordlessly she nodded, turning away to stare blindly over the sea. If she said anything more—even just his name—she'd howl like a baby, and she had too much pride to do that.

In a voice completely devoid of emotion, he went on, 'I don't think it would be a good idea for you to visit the king right now. When this comes out—and it will, even if it's only innuendo and insinuations—there'll be a constitutional crisis. It will be better for everyone if you're not mixed up in it. The jet will take you back to New Zealand.'

She said thinly, 'All right.'

He didn't touch her, but as she turned to go back to the villa he said deliberately, 'Rosa, I'm sorry. But I'll never be sorry for these last few days.'

Incredibly, she managed a smile. 'Neither will I,' she said, and walked back to the villa and started to pack.

He saw her once more as the helicopter landed on the beach to take her back to Porto di Castellante. He was waiting outside the bedroom door, and as she came out he said quietly, 'Goodbye, sweet Rosa.'

Tears aching in her throat, she made a muffled sound and turned away. 'Goodbye. And—thank you.'

His hand on her shoulder stilled her. Hardly daring to breathe, she obeyed its summons and looked up into his face. He looked older, his face drawn and darkly intimidating, no softness, no hint of compromise in the autocratic features. He bent his head and kissed her forehead.

'You will make a superb queen. Be happy.'

'Will you be?' she asked fiercely, refusing to accept platitudes.

His mouth tightened. 'I believe that eventually even the greatest grief is eased by time.'

'Do you?' she said simply. 'Goodbye, Max.'

By the time the jet delivered her to New Zealand, the news had well and truly broken. Even on that side of the world the papers devoted a lot of space to juicy descriptions of the turmoil in the richest royal family in the world. The more serious press explored the constitutional crisis, but the popular magazines and papers concentrated on the scanty details of Queen Eva's long-ago affair with Giovanni, splashing them across the pages accompanied by photographs of all of the heirs who'd turned down the throne.

But nowhere, neither in New Zealand nor

overseas, was there a whisper about the precious days she'd spent with Max.

Although several stringers for foreign news agencies hung around her flat for a couple of days, they gave up when she and Kate refused any comments.

Her immediate family were constantly supportive by both email and on the telephone, while agreeing that she was in the best place, as far from the chaos as she could be. In one brief, formal call her grandfather requested that she give no interviews. He'd brushed off her enquiries about his health with a few curt words.

The wider Niroli royal family—and those who had recently believed themselves royal—closed ranks and stayed silent. The palace refused comment.

No one at the lab mentioned the scandal, although her boss called her in and suggested awkwardly that she might take time off as she'd been looking a bit tired recently.

She refused, but each morning saw her apply a layer of concealer beneath her eyes and boost the intensity of her lipstick, and on the really bad nights she took half a sleeping pill.

Not long after she'd arrived back in New Zealand, Rosa threw a newspaper—one that featured an interview with a distant cousin of Giovanni's wife—to one side, uttering a very rude word indeed.

'Cheer up,' Kate said bracingly, 'it could have been worse. At least nobody's been killed in all this fuss, and as far as I can see there's been no hint of drugs or child slavery in it either.'

Rosa gave a pale grin. 'Not vices the ruling house of Niroli dabble in,' she said bleakly.

'Good on them. And you seem to have scotched the blight outbreak in Niroli. How's your research coming along?'

'Fine.' It was a mechanical answer.

Kate raised her brows, but said nothing more about Niroli, for which Rosa was very grateful.

She'd known that missing Max would be difficult.

Oh, she'd known *nothing*, she thought passionately.

Life without him was empty of savour, a bland, featureless existence that stretched ahead, dreary day after dreary day until the end of her life. At night she ached for him, longing for something—some indication that he hadn't forgotten her, that they really had shared those sunlit days and long, hot nights when he'd taught her how to be a woman.

His woman.

Even at work the zest, the fascination with science that had always gone with her previously, had packed its bags and departed, along with her heart and her happiness. It had been so easy to say that whatever happened they'd have those days to remember, but she'd had no idea how bitterly sweet the memories would be.

And although she was worried about the succession to the throne, she couldn't concentrate on it. It didn't matter that neither her grandfather nor anyone from the palace secretariat had contacted her again; if she ended up on the throne of Niroli she'd do her best, just as she'd always done. She hoped that would be enough.

Turning her head, Kate said sharply, 'Someone's coming up the path—I'll see who they are.'

When she came back in she looked disturbed. 'Reporters. Do you want to see them?'

'God, no.'

The telephone rang. Kate snatched it up and

listened, her face settling into what she called the standard legal expression of noncommittal blandness. 'Can you prove that?' she asked.

CHAPTER TWELVE

AFTER a pause Kate frowned, took the receiver from her ear and covered the mouthpiece with her hand. 'He says he's your grandfather's private secretary.'

Rosa dragged in a deep breath as she lifted the telephone to her ear. Briefly, the king's right-hand man told her that Max was no longer the heir to the throne, and asked her to keep herself ready for anything that might happen. She was not to speak to the press.

Numbly she agreed to everything, but when she went to put the receiver back her hand was shaking so badly she dropped it, and gave a startled sob.

Kate came flying back in, but stopped after one look at Rosa's face. 'I'll make you coffee,' she said.

It came with a stiff shot of brandy. 'Drink it,'

Kate commanded. 'What the hell is your family doing to you?'

Another knock on the door drove her to the window. 'Bloody reporters,' she muttered. 'Something's happened—they've got that baying-for-blood look. Do you feel like telling me what's going on?'

Rosa nodded and sketchily, without mentioning her feelings, filled her in on the situation.

Kate pursed her lips, saying after a pause heavy with unspoken thoughts, 'I think I could do with a brandy too.'

'It's probably a good idea,' Rosa said wearily. 'Let's just not talk about it, OK?'

'OK by me, but if you want to, I'm here.'

In spite of Kate's support, she had never felt so alone in her life. She spent a sleepless night staring into an intolerable future. When she came into the kitchen the next morning Kate eyed her up and down and exclaimed, 'You're not going to work, are you?'

'Why not? The reporters have gone.'

Kate hesitated, then said, 'It looks like it, but I bet they'll be back as soon as they've had breakfast.'

She was right; they arrived in a pack the moment Rosa closed the gates behind the car and hurled questions at her as she got back into it.

'How do you feel about the scandal in the family?' the most pushy woman demanded, microphone at the ready. 'Did you know about Queen Eva's affair with the gardener?'

Sickened, Rosa groped for the handle of the door to close it, but their questions beat against her.

'Is the king going to divorce her?'

'How do you feel about your cousins not really being your cousins?'

'Are you going to be the next ruler of Niroli?'

Harried and furious, Rosa drove off, narrowly missing a not-too-alert television cameraman, but after a distracted day trying to concentrate on her work had to fight her way back into the house.

The telephone rang again that night, once more with the king's private secretary on the other end. 'We have tried to keep your privacy as our first consideration,' he stated austerely, as though it were her fault reporters had camped outside her house, 'but rumours have begun to circulate suggesting that you're to be the next ruler.

Because this leaves you vulnerable, a security firm has been contacted; they should be arriving any minute to take you to a lodge in South Island.'

'I see,' she said woodenly. 'Thank you.'

She wanted to ask him where Max was, what was happening. Instead, she hung up and told Kate what was happening.

'About time too,' her friend said vigorously. 'Will you be all right? Do you want me to contact your sister or anyone else in your family?'

'No, I'll be fine. I'll ring you tonight,' Rosa said, trying to sound casual. 'If my cousin Max gets in touch—which is highly unlikely—can you give him my cellphone number?'

Kate promised to do that, and offered to help her pack.

Four hours later she was ensconced in a magnificent private lodge halfway up a mountain on the long alpine spine of the South Island. Facing her was the man who'd smuggled her out of the house and into a plane; solid, middle-aged, efficient and friendly, he was telling her of the measures they'd taken to ensure both her privacy and her safety.

He'd covered everything—even gone to the lab and got enough work to keep her occupied.

'Thank you for everything,' she said, trying very hard to sound her usual self.

He shrugged and smiled. 'I was told you'd rather leave than have bodyguards and try to go about your normal routine.'

She was surprised her grandfather knew enough about her to understand that, but the information warmed her heart. In spite of everything, it seemed he was thinking of her.

The lodge must have been entirely taken over by the king, because no other guests disturbed her solitude during the two long weeks that followed. Isabella emailed frequently, as did her brothers, but they were locked out of Niroli's affairs. The newspapers were filled with endless speculation, in which Adam Ryder's name wasn't mentioned. No one knew where Max was.

And Kate rang each day to tell her that Max hadn't tried to contact her.

Spring in the mountains was beautiful. Her host and hostess were charming, interesting people who kept finding intriguing things for her to do. Rosa did her best to appear to enjoy it. When she wasn't working, or obsessively following what was being reported about the situation on Niroli, she went for long walks with an amiable black and white sheepdog that seemed as fascinated as she was by the high country. She thought much about the way shot blight managed to survive in a world that did its best to kill it.

And she pined like a Victorian maiden abandoned by her lover. It was ridiculous; she'd known right from the start that she and Max could never hope for any sort of happy ending, but that knowledge didn't forestall the aching emptiness that lay in wait for her every hour of every day.

And pounced during the long, bitter nights.

Doggedly, she kept working, taking her laptop outside to enjoy the crisp, golden air beside the pool, noting the tide of activity on a working sheep station.

One afternoon the sound of a helicopter intruded into the solitude. Getting to her feet, she watched as it settled behind the trees that sheltered the house, and allowed a moment's hope. Her stomach knotted and she braced herself.

Was this a messenger from the king, calling her back to Niroli and the throne? Or had he found someone else?

Except that there was no one else.

Jaw set, panic kicking in her stomach, she walked into the house and up to her bedroom. Whatever, she planned to be properly dressed.

By the time someone knocked at the door of her luxurious suite she was clad in linen trousers and a white shirt, her feet in high-heeled sandals, cosmetics masking her pallor.

'Come in,' she said quietly, so quietly she had to clear her throat and repeat it with more emphasis.

The door opened, and she gave a shocked, incredulous gasp, because it was Max who stood there.

She clamped down on her first instinct, to run to him and throw herself into his arms, but her gaze clung hungrily to his dark, arrogant features.

'Rosa,' he said, his hooded gaze intent and purposeful.

She swallowed. 'Did he know how cruel of him it was to send you?'

He realised instantly what she meant. 'Your

grandfather didn't send me,' he said, and came inside and closed the door behind him.

Eyes enormous in a face more angular, subtly thinner, she gazed at him. 'Then it was cruel of you to come,' she whispered.

'The nightmare's over for both of us,' Max said, furious all over again with the old man whose stubbornness had put her through such hell. He frowned at the bewilderment in her face. 'We're free,' he told her, triumph colouring the words.

'I don't understand…'

'Free to do anything we want. I'm no longer the heir and neither are you.'

She frowned. 'Then who is?'

'Adam Ryder,' he said, anger edging his tone. 'Haven't they told you anything?'

'Who?'

'Those grey old men at the palace.' He clamped down on his fury, forcing himself to think calmly. She looked as though she'd been on the wire too long, so strung out she could barely take in what he was saying. More gently he said, 'Sit down, my sweet girl.'

She looked around vaguely before collapsing into a chair over by the window. 'You must be tired if you've just arrived in New Zealand,' she said with a return of colour to her cheeks. She gestured to another chair. 'Tell me what's been happening.'

He lowered himself down, wishing he could just sit and take her in. But her eyes were fixed onto his face with an intensity that produced a fresh surge of cold fury in him. 'What exactly do you know of the events at the palace?' he asked.

'Nothing,' she said simply. 'I was just told not to talk to the press, and then, later, that as rumours were circulating about me being the next ruler it was deemed safer to bring me here.'

He swore richly and fluently, and she started to laugh, only to choke it back because tears threatened to overwhelm her.

'My poor girl,' he said harshly. 'If I'd known that they were keeping you in the dark I'd have rung night and morning to keep you up to date with negotiations. Tell me one thing—do you want to be Queen?'

She stared at him with horror. 'No. Never. Max, you know that—why do you even bother to ask?'

'Because I've spent the time since you left

Niroli bargaining with the king on that assumption. Perhaps I should have made sure you hadn't changed your mind—'

'Why?' she said, bewildered all over again. 'You didn't need to ask me again. Max, if you don't tell me what's happened, I'll—I'll hit you!'

'I'm sorry, I'm making a mess of this.' He smiled without amusement, and ran a hand over his chin, briefly closing his eyes. 'In short, once the king understood that I don't have a drop of Fierrezza blood in me, he decided that you could be whipped into shape as an acceptable queen. He even picked out a perfectly good husband for you—one who'd actually rule the country. So I spent some of the more arduous days of my life persuading him that Adam Ryder would be a better choice.'

She stared at him, reading more than he intended in the hard features. The negotiations had been hard-fought, probably antagonistic. Her heart began to pick up speed. 'Why?'

'Because it was the only thing I could do for you,' he said soberly. 'In the end he capitulated, after I told him that you and I were lovers, and that you could already be pregnant. The thought of another scandal was more than he could cope with.'

'Is he all right?' she asked swiftly, using her concern for her grandfather to hide the shivering pleasure that had swept over her at the thought of carrying Max's baby.

His smile was ironic yet subtly respectful. 'He's fine. And when I pointed out to him that there is no actual rule that says the heirs to the throne of Niroli must be legitimate, I think he was relieved. I was helped by the fact that the palace hierarchy agreed that Adam was a better bet, more agreeable to the islanders than a woman would ever be.'

Exultation soared, then died. He'd fought for her freedom, but that didn't mean that he loved her. Very evenly she said, 'That was kind of you. And there is no baby.'

'I'm glad of that.' He was watching her closely, hard green-gold eyes shadowed by heavy lashes, his mouth a little grim. 'I'd hate to see you made tabloid fodder. You called me kind once before. I don't feel kindly where you're concerned, Rosa. I told the king about—us—because it seemed to me that taking my own freedom by casting you to the wolves was the act of a coward.' His eyelids dropped until his eyes were narrow slivers of pure green. 'But if you do want power, it's not too late. I suspect the king would still prefer a legitimate scion of his house to inherit rather than Adam.'

Without pausing for thought, she said passionately, 'I feel just the same as I did before. I'd have taken it on because there's no one else and I thought it my duty, but it would have been hell.'

His response didn't come immediately. And when it did, she couldn't believe it. In a level, uninflected voice, he said, 'I think I fell in love with you when you were sixteen, but it was impossible—not only were we cousins, but you were far too young. So I buried it deep. However, I must always have thought that eventually, when you were grown-up, we could meet as equals and go on from there. When I realised I'd have to take on the throne, my first, strongest reaction blew me away. It was so damned unexpected—anger because it meant that we'd never get our chance. But at last I'm free to ask you to marry me. If that's what you want.'

Rosa scrambled to her feet, searching his formidable face for some clue to his emotions. 'You don't have to offer,' she blurted. She clenched her fists and took the greatest gamble of her life. 'Is that what you want?'

Very quietly, he said, 'I want it more than I have wanted anything else in my life—but you're still very young. I don't want to over-persuade you into thinking you love me because I'm the first man to give you an orgasm.'

Cheeks burning, she said in a shaken voice, 'I'm not so stupidly naive. I love you, but I won't tie you to a marriage you don't want because you feel some sort of obligation to me.'

'Obligation?' He gave a short, fierce laugh and in his unguarded eyes she saw a flash of need so great it hurt her heart.

'There is no sense of obligation,' he said in a tough, implacable voice. 'I have never lied to you, and I'm not lying now when I tell you that I love you. I'm confident of my own feelings; I'm not confident of yours. Romance and love are two different things, Rosa; one is delicious but fleeting, the other is bedrock. You must be sure—'

'Of course I'm sure,' she broke in, terrified she

wouldn't be able to convince him. 'Until I went to Niroli again I—yes, I romanticised my feelings for you, hero-worshipped you. But seeing you as the man you are, not some fairy-tale prince, made me realise just how—how magnificent you are, how strong and how worthy of admiration and respect. I learned to love you properly then, when you helped the growers haul out their vines and supported them and were their anchor and their hope.'

She searched his face, her heart racing, trying to discern some hint of his reaction. It came as a glimmer of gold in the green eyes, and a smile, not the tender smile of a lover but the fierce tri-umphant joy of a winner.

Hope flared high in her, and then a joy to match his—equally consuming, equally elemental.

Even then he didn't take a step towards her. In a voice she'd never heard before, he said, 'As I found you, my heart—utterly magnificent in your dedication and your compassion. Rosa, my own true love, will you be my wife? We can live in New Zealand and set up a wine empire, and our children will grow up free of all the stresses and constraints of being royalty.'

When he saw tears gather in her huge, mysterious eyes, he said in a shaken voice, 'Sweetheart, don't cry. Don't ever cry again. Just say yes.'

'Yes,' she whispered. 'Of course I'll marry you—of course I'll live here with you. Max, I love you so much—I thought you'd forgotten me. Why aren't you holding me?'

'If I touch you we'll never get this said, and I think it needs to be,' he said, irony colouring his voice. 'But I could never forget you. Never. You've been in the forefront of my mind every second that we've been parted. You always will be.'

And at last he moved, and she ran into his arms, shivering with a feverish mixture of excitement and relief as they closed around her, warm and strong and safe. 'Now kiss me,' he said unevenly. 'I'm starving for you.'

Torn between laughter and tears, Rosa raised her lips and kissed him, her mouth lingering against his, her whole being clamouring exultantly for the passionate consummation only he could give her. He lifted his head, and she saw the dark flush of colour along his arrogant cheekbones, met his intense, narrowed stare, and then gulped as the room whirled and he carried her across to the huge bed.

Much later, lying exhausted in his arms, she said dreamily, 'When I recover I'm going to plague you with more questions, but just now I don't care about anything but us.'

'Mmm,' he said, his voice roughly tender. 'Me too. You, and our future.'

After another very satisfactory interlude, she asked, 'How did you find me? Did my grandfather tell you where I was?'

'No, I had to tell him.'

Her drooping lashes flicked up and she scanned his beloved face. 'What?'

'This is my house, my land.' His eyes narrowed. 'His idea of protection was to sequester you in a high-security hotel and give you bodyguards. I knew you'd be miserable, so I organised it with my security to bring you here. Fortunately, his secretary agreed to ring you and tell you as though the order came from the king. I suspected that you wouldn't come if you knew it was my doing.'

She digested this in silence, and then sighed. 'I should have known,' she said simply, and kissed him with an overflowing heart. 'You know me well—I've loved it here.' Well, she would have if she'd known the station belonged to Max. 'What's going to happen to Niroli's vines?'

He shrugged. 'I appointed a new head to replace me—Giovanni's grandson.' He was silent for a moment, then said, 'My cousin.'

'Do I know him?'

'Probably not. I'm proud of my new family. I head-hunted him from a very successful career in Australia. He's a good man, and he'll take Niroli into the future.'

'Good.' She yawned. 'This seems like a miracle,' she said sleepily, exhaustion dragging her into sleep.

He rolled over onto his back. 'Hardly,' he said drily. 'The king tried to persuade me to say nothing and marry you.'

Stunned, Rosa sat bolt upright and fixed him with an incredulous stare. 'Did he? Were *you* the husband he picked for me? Why didn't you?'

He shrugged, sleek brown skin still slightly damp from their love-making. 'It would be living a lie. He wanted a quick marriage between us, so that when the scandal actually broke he could present the islanders with a *fait accompli*.'

'In other words, he intended you to be de facto ruler, with me providing the Fierezza blood and just being a figurehead and baby factory.'

'He did indeed,' he said grimly. 'From his point of view, a satisfactory conclusion. And he was probably right. A marriage, plus the fact that you were going to be next Queen of Niroli, would have trumped the scandal.'

'I'm glad you said no.'

He reached out a long arm and hooked her down on top of him. His eyes searched hers, probing and hard. 'Why?'

'Because I'd have married you—of course I'd have married you!—but I want a normal life for us and our children, one that doesn't revolve around pomp and protocol. I want to be able to keep up my career, even though I know I won't be able to be at the cutting edge of research—'

His intimidating intensity faded into warm understanding. 'My dearest love, you won't have to give anything up. I'll build you a full-scale lab.' His smile held just enough relief for her to realise that he'd been concerned how she'd feel about his refusal to take on the kingdom. 'One in every house we own so you can work on whatever you want to.'

Grinning, she said, 'Well, shot blight to start off with. Although I'll be almost sorry to crack it, because it brought us together.'

'Ah, no,' he said, and kissed her naked shoulder. 'That would have happened sooner or later. We were meant for each other.'

'No more worries about being years older than me?' she teased.

He grinned self-derisively. 'None. It was only ever a desperate attempt to shore up my defences, and it failed miserably.'

Laughing, she hugged him, but quickly sobered. 'Do you think Adam Ryder will agree to be the next heir?'

'Once I refused it the king refused to discuss any matters of state with me, but I suspect Adam has already consented.'

She said quietly, 'I see. I hope it works out.' And then she gave a voluptuous little wriggle. 'I'm so relieved it's over and that we don't have to worry anymore. What happens next?'

'Hell!' Max sat up, dislodging her. He looked

around, saw his trousers in a heap on the floor and turned to her with amusement and heat lighting his eyes. 'I meant to give you something before we went to bed! I wonder if you're always going to have this interesting effect on me.'

'I hope so,' she said demurely, but her smug smile faded when he reached for the discarded garment and took out a small black box.

Almost diffidently, he said, 'I don't know whether or not you want this as an engagement ring, but I saw it a couple of years ago and bought it for you.'

'For me?' She stared at him. 'Two years ago? But you didn't—we didn't…'

'I always hoped,' he said with raw decisiveness. 'Always—until our parents died, and then one by one the heirs started to refuse the throne. I thought that everyone else would be able to marry for love except us, yet I still hoped.'

He flicked the box open, and she whispered on an indrawn breath, 'Oh, Max! It's utterly beautiful!'

'It's a rose diamond,' he said. 'For your name. And it's heart-shaped, for my heart.'

He picked it out of the box and held it out. Eyes filling with tears, Rosa held out her hand, so that he could slide the exquisite thing onto her finger.

He kissed her hand, and then the ring, and said deeply, 'It's just a token. It's probably too big to wear on a daily basis so we'll buy another, more sensible one, but over the years it's given me hope that we could overcome the obstacles.'

'It's not just a token!' she scolded. 'And, no, you won't buy me another one! I'll always cherish it, because it means that you never gave up hope that somehow we'd be together.'

He shrugged. 'Hope was all I had. So, when are you going to marry me?'

'Whenever and wherever you like,' she said, and punched him in the ribs with one serviceable fist.

'What the hell—?' He grabbed her hand and examined her knuckles, his eyes narrowed and dangerous. 'What was that for?'

'For not telling me that you loved me before you sent me away!' Tears welled up into her eyes. 'I thought I was never going to see you again. You must have known I loved you, but you never said it!'

He groaned and kissed her fingers, then pulled her into his arms and rocked her as she wept away the trauma of the past weeks, the pain and the loneliness and the grief.

In the end he said, 'Hush, my treasure, my darling one, hush! I didn't tell you then because I thought it would make it so much harder for you. I knew that I'd never marry, but I hoped that one day you'd find someone else to love, and I suspected that your faithful heart would prevent it if you knew that for me there would never be any other woman. Dry your eyes and let me see you smile.'

She hiccuped and blew her nose and said reluctantly, 'You were probably right, but, oh, it's been a wretched time.' She looked into his face. 'Not as wretched as it's been for you, though.'

'I had something to occupy my mind,' he said drily. 'Your grandfather is a tough negotiator. He sends you his love, by the way, and says he wants our first son to be named after him.'

'Giorgio?' She blushed profusely, and laughed. 'The old rogue!'

And lay back on the bed to look into her future, with everything she'd been prepared to give up safely held fast. But nothing, she thought dreamily as he kissed the top of her head, would ever take Max's place in her heart—not her work, nor Niroli.

She'd had a short time to experience life without him; shuddering, she clung to his hard, warm body and vowed to thank every day whatever benign destiny had manipulated events so that they had reached this rapturous felicity together.

* * * * *

Chaos ensues on Niroli as all the legitimate Fierezza heirs are ruled out. Now a outsider with royal blood is the country's only chance of continuing years of tradition, but unbeknownst to the royal house another man can lay claim to the throne...

THE mirror mocked him.

He recognised the body, but the person escaped him. Water glistened in rivulets as it trickled down the torso of his reflection. His nakedness became his only truth. The desert clothes he held slipped from his grasp to the floor unwanted, unneeded...discarded. The shoulders that had taken endless beatings from the fierce desert heat stood broad, flexed, waiting for their next burden, their next challenge. A different heat. A Nirolian heat. Soon, the Nirolian sun would kiss his honeyed skin, scold his blackened brow, and lick its way into his mind.

The desert robes would stay, discarded on the floor.

'Fetch me the suit.' He glanced momentarily towards his manservant. His hooded eyes betrayed nothing of the battle raging within him.

As he dressed he knew the transformation was beginning... The crisp white shirt and coal-black jacket fell effortlessly from him, caressing the muscles it encased. The dark tailored trousers created the perfect silhouette of a man ready to rule. He rolled his shoulders, adjusting to the weight of his new uniform.

Turning, he raised his dark eyes up to meet his reflection. No longer mocking, the mirror bowed down to him, worshipped him, it paid its penance and captured his glory, his essence. He was ready.

* * * * *

Plans are afoot and although our mystery sheikh has never set foot on Niroli he has Fierezza blood running through his veins.
Find out who will triumph in
BRIDE BY ROYAL APPOINTMENT,
book seven in The Royal House of Niroli!